A Different Kind of Light

First published in Great Britain in 2021 by Black Shuck Books

Cover design by WHITEspace
Set in Caslon by WHITEspace
www.white-space.uk

978-1-913038-61-8

A Different Kind of Light

by
Simon Bestwick

BLACK
SHUCK
BOOKS

*These flickers and frames
are for Gemma Files*

I met Danielle Starmer at Hull University in the late '90s, when we were both studying History there. We fell in and out of bed several times over the next few years – we liked one another, and the sex was incredible, but our one attempt at cohabitation lasted a bare fortnight. We remained friends, nonetheless, and occasionally still fucked. It was one of the odder relationships I've had.

We both graduated with solid degrees and put them to good use. I became (ultimately) a freelance researcher and I earned a living at it. I didn't think I'd done too badly for an awkward Pakistani boy from the wrong end of Bradford, even if lads I'd grown up with were earning more money: I had my independence, and that counted for a lot. Danie started at the BBC, advising on their endless costume dramas. When it became clear that she knew more about the relevant topics than her employers, she struck out on her own as well, setting up a costume and properties company which soon became one of the leading ones in the field.

We stayed in touch, but mostly by email and the occasional video-call; we hadn't met face to face in the better part of a decade when she called last October.

"Ash? Danie." Brisk and to the point as ever; for moment I was in the bedroom in her old digs in

Hull. Lie back, she'd say. Arms above your head. Now do this. Now that. Some people reveal their hidden selves in bed – like the alpha male likes to be tied up and whipped – but Danie was the same all the way through; she liked to be in control, in everything. "How are you? Good, great. I'm okay. Listen, what's your diary like this week? Clear? Good. Listen, how'd you fancy a trip down South? All expenses paid? Well – got something you might be interested in. Tell you more when you get here. Friday, then? See you soon. Can't wait. Bye, bye, bye."

And so, a few days after Hurricane Danie had left me blinking dazedly with a dead phone in my hand, my train pulled into Euston Station.

I *can* drive, but for long journeys I've always preferred the train; my attention tends to wander on long trips. I like gazing out of the windows and enjoying the view, which isn't exactly recommended if you're in charge of a moving vehicle. Besides which, motorways these days scare the hell out of me, and the prospect of dealing with the M25 was enough to turn my hair white.

There'd been a couple of delays on the way down from Sheffield: a brownout near Loughborough, and what the radio had euphemistically called 'unrest' had halted us on the approach to Luton. On top of that the catering car was empty and the toilet in my carriage wasn't. It was also broken, as was the lock on its door, which meant that it swung constantly open and shut, wafting its fragrance throughout the train.

I was glad to get out of the carriage and onto the platform – travelling light with my compact backpack – only to be brought up short by the state of the place. Euston had never been a beauty spot, but now the floor was thick with discarded food wrappers, chicken bones, even pigeon carcasses. The worst of the refuse had been swept into corners, to fester in heaps. In summer the stench would have been unbearable. Danie told me later that the cleaning company had gone under and a frantic hunt for a replacement was underway.

Outside the station, between me and the taxi rank, sat a line of homeless people, most of them with the gaunt, grey look of addicts. Across the street, a row of prostitutes lounged against the wall, blowing kisses and calling out to any men whose eye they caught. They were haggard and feral-looking, with scabbed lips and matted hair; the only responses they inspired were pity and revulsion.

The taxi rank reeked of urine, excrement, and the foetor of long-unwashed human bodies: rank by name, rank by nature. I tried not to catch any of the beggars' eyes; I always do. Being a freelancer, I never feel far enough from where they are. I always dread seeing someone I know.

The taxis were few and far between, but at last one came; I scrambled gratefully aboard and gave Danie's address to the driver. His English was minimal, and it took nearly five minutes to establish where I wanted to go and for him to find it on his satnav. Finally he pulled out and I slumped back in my seat, although I didn't fully relax until we pulled into Barrowford Row.

Danie's house, a three-storey Georgian mid-terrace in Islington, was a trendy enough location, but at least half the properties there were up for sale or rent. Most of the residents worked in the media sector, which had taken a pounding in recent months due to the latest round of cuts and belt-tightening. Approaching her door after paying off the taxi driver, I was irrationally certain that she too would be gone, pulled under by the sudden undertow of a bankruptcy since we'd last talked.

But she answered the door on the first knock as if she'd been waiting there all night, barefoot in jeans and a black vest top, toenails painted bright electric blue.

"Ashok Dhillon, you old goat." She kissed my cheek, gave me a hug.

I laughed. "Less of the old."

"Get yourself in before the natives eat you."

I hoped she was joking – I'd seen a news story about a cannibalism in Acton the week before – but when I was inside she fastened three different locks, pulled a deadbolt across and fitted a security chain. "Wine? Dinner'll be ready any minute – I've had a chilli in the crockpot all day."

"Sounds great." Danie's kitchen repertoire ranged from curry through Bolognese and chilli – based on which herbs and spices she used (or in the chilli's case, whether she threw in a can of kidney beans) – but it was always palatable and plentiful. The rice had been steaming away in another cooker, and there was a bowl each of nachos, salsa and sour cream.

"Red or white?"

"Red, please."

Danie poured us each a glass, then flopped onto the sofa and put her feet up on the coffee table. Her soles were grubby. She'd never liked shoes or socks, and went without them whenever she could. She'd had much the same attitude towards clothes in general when we'd first met, I recalled, and immediately wrenched my mind away from the topic. Danie had always been far better at getting over me than the other way around.

"So," I said, "what's the big secret?"

Danie smiled crookedly and shook her head. "Tomorrow."

"Seriously?"

She shrugged and gave her glass a swirl. "I need your unbiased opinion, Ash. I mean, *really* important."

"Life and death?"

She grimaced. "Close enough."

Danie looked more frazzled than I'd seen her in years. I thought of the other houses along Barrowford Row with their For Sale and To Let signs, and guessed she hadn't escaped the latest round of industry body-blows completely unscathed. If I'd looked in the right places, I think I'd have found a mountain of unpaid bills. People in that situation do stupid things; illegal, even. But a lot of people were in that boat; the only reason I wasn't was sheer luck, that and a pretty frugal existence in a cottage on the Yorkshire Moors I'd more or less hand-restored from total dereliction. Even then, I'd come close on occasion – more than close, a couple of times.

Even now, I'm not sure Danie saw all that, but I think she saw enough to know that I knew. She looked afraid, and an ugly part of me wondered what she'd be willing to do in exchange for my help. I told it to shut up, wondering as I did if this was why I'd always been less successful than Danie, and if my lack of ruthlessness would doom me to end my days begging outside Euston Station, stinking like an open sewer.

"Can't you tell me anything?" I said.

"I'd rather not. You've been travelling all day, you must be exhausted. I want fresh eyes on this, and—"

"Unbiased."

"Unbiased." She clinked her glass to mine.

"Okay," I said, "so, in the morning?"

"Yup. meantime, let's eat."

I had no argument with that. And so we ate chilli, smoked a joint she rolled – Danie's responsibility since our college years, when she'd regularly referred to my efforts at skinning up as 'an elephant's Tampax' – and watched a double bill of trashy DVDs. By then we were sitting together on the sofa, and it felt very like old times. Which wasn't so bad; there'd been no freefalling economy back then, no food riots, no brownouts. Pension at sixty-five and far fewer maniacs in power. We'd sat around the student's union smoking (you could smoke indoors in those days, too), bitching about the state of the world, but we'd have had that world back in a heartbeat if we could.

At the end of the second film, Danie held out a hand, helped me up off the sofa and led me upstairs to her room. I've no idea whether she did so for fun, or for old times' sake. Or just to ensure I was on-side. I'd like to think that it wasn't that. I'd also like to think that my refusal to exploit her need for my help influenced her decision.

But as Danie would have been the first to tell you, I always was naïve.

"Basically," she said over breakfast the following morning, "I want you to authenticate something."

Breakfast was bacon rolls – cheap, salty bacon, and possibly on the turn – and instant coffee, both of which would have been anathema to Danie even two years before. It seemed to confirm my conjecture of the night before.

"How come you need my help on this?" I said. "You're every bit as good as I am."

"Better."

"And so modest."

"You were always better at *that*," she admitted, "but then you had so much more to be modest *about*."

Ouch. "But you still need me for this?"

I was afraid she'd tell me that I was a charity case, some sort of Girl Guide good deed on her part, but she didn't seem to be in a position to dispense charity. Danie sighed and raised a hand. "All right. This is sort of off the books, okay? Commission for a private client. Locate an item, confirm it's the genuine article, then deliver it."

"And before you splash out on it you want to make sure, or the client might not pay up and you'll be in an even bigger hole."

Danie reddened. I felt guilty; I'd sounded harsher than I'd meant. Cruel, even. "Sorry."

"Whatever. You *are* getting a cut, you know. I'm not asking you to work for free."

Danie's a proud woman. She'd probably hoped I'd be too polite to mention her circumstances. I should have been. She was hanging onto her dignity by her badly-bitten fingernails. I was tempted to assure her that it wasn't the money, that for a good friend I'd give up my time for free, but I didn't. Danie might well have taken me up on the offer, and I had some pride too.

"So, what do you need my special skills for? Antique porn?"

"I wish."

"Seriously?"

She half-smiled, but then it faded. "Look – I'll get it for you, and you can see for yourself. I want—"

"My unbiased opinion?"

"Yeah."

———

Danie shooed me into the living room with another mug of Aldi's finest and ran upstairs. She came back down with a DVD in a plain jewel case. There was something written on the disc, but she didn't let me see what. She pulled the curtains and dimmed the lights. "Okay," she said, "see what you make of this."

The DVD played. The picture was black and white, and it looked like old newsreel footage. A motor racetrack, with stands of closely packed spectators, far too close to the track. Closer than they'd ever be allowed these days, ever since…

I looked more closely at the screen. Racing cars swept past – Jags, Mercedes-Benzes, a Cunningham C6-R; Triumphs and Ferraris, Aston-Martins, Maseratis. I looked closer still, and made out the number plate of an oncoming vehicle. An Austin-Healey 100: NOJ 393.

My forearms prickled, and the back of my neck, because that was when I understood what I was watching. I knew, even though the footage was in black and white, that the Austin-Healey was painted

British Racing Green. I knew also that the driver was a thirty-six year old Englishman called Lance Macklin, and that the D-Type Jaguar in front of him was driven by a twenty-five year old playboy called Mike Hawthorn. I knew, as well, that the man driving of the Mercedes 300 SLR behind Macklin was a forty-nine-year-old Frenchman called Pierre Levegh, and that behind him, in another Merc, was Juan-Manuel Fangio, who many still considered the greatest racing driver of all time.

And although I'd never seen it from this particular angle, I knew what was coming next.

Hawthorn's Jag veered towards the pits, cutting across Macklin's path and slowing down. Macklin swerved and braked to avoid a collision; he barely made it. Levegh made a hand signal that gave Fangio, behind him, enough warning to slow down and change course; Fangio would later say he owed his life to Levegh.

Another second and Levegh, too, might have had time to stop or take evasive action. But he didn't have another second; at over eighty miles per hour, you rarely do.

The Mercedes' front right wheel rode up over the Austin Healey's left rear corner, as if up a ramp; Macklin went slewing sideways, fighting for control, but you never notice that on any of the films. What you notice is Levegh's car going airborne and rolling end over end for two hundred and sixty feet towards the terraces and grandstand, before bouncing off the earth embankment and exploding as it smashes into a concrete stairwell.

I'd watched footage of the crash and its aftermath several times before, always with the same appalled, sick fascination. The car on fire; smoke boiling up from the stands; Levegh lying by the car, his clothes burning. The other cars racing by as match officials and ambulancemen ran towards the crash site. I'd seen all that before; I *hadn't* seen what came next.

The picture lurched; the frame swung downwards, to point at the ground. Then the camera was in motion, bouncing – a pair of running feet darted in and out of shot – and the turf gave way to the tarmacked surface of the track.

Smoke. Blood. Firemarks. The camera zoomed in on Levegh's body, then pulled back. Fire filled the screen for a moment, cold and brilliant in the black and white. The cameraman skirted round it and through the ruined barriers into the stands.

I'd heard about what the rescuers had witnessed, but I'd never seen it. Not until now.

Levegh's Mercedes had exploded, almost literally, like a bomb – a combination of shrapnel and incendiary. The hood of the car had sheared through the crowd like a guillotine blade; the axle, white-hot from the explosion, had done the same. The SLR had been built from magnesium alloy for lightness: once ignited, it blazed, incandescent, for hours.

The camera wove through the dead, then halted. It took me a few dazed and startled seconds to process the sight.

Most of them were children. They sat motionless, even with the flames roaring yards away. Many still clutched ice-cream cornets in their hands, and all of them were headless. Somehow the images were far worse in black and white than they would have been in colour.

I heard the click of Danie's old brass Zippo lighter, and caught the tang of cigarette smoke. Plain tobacco, not even a joint; she hardly ever did that. I glanced at her; she sat with her back to me, facing the window. The smoke glowed in the thin light from outside.

I turned back to the screen. The camera panned back and forth across the bodies, till several of them toppled over: a man in a suit, collar askew, hair wild, picked up one of the children and staggered away with the body. It looked as if he was talking to the child.

The cameraman continued to film, feeding the camera's greedy eye with more bodies, more wounds.

Le Mans, 11th June, 1955. More than eighty people died that day, including Pierre Levegh, whose badly burned body could only be recovered when his wrecked car had burned itself out. The final death toll is still disputed. Seasoned photographers who'd covered wars and murders were shaken by the footage they'd captured. Most of it, for obvious reasons, had never seen the light of day.

I let the footage play out, then found the remote and restarted the recording, powering up my laptop. This was one of the reasons Danie and I had never worked as a couple. Unhealthy curiosity, she calls it, on my part, about the kind of stuff we don't normally get to see. Morbid. Well, we all have our odd little obsessions.

As I began making notes, Danie got up and left the room.

I went to the kitchen in search of coffee and broke out in a coughing fit as I walked into a wall of tobacco smoke.

"Sorry." Danie turned the fan above the kitchen range on and opened the patio. The dull October wind turned the kitchen cold, but at least the air was clear.

"It's the real deal," I told her.

"I'm skinning up. Want a toke?"

"Did you hear what I said?"

"Yes. Toke?"

"Okay. Brew?"

"Please."

I brought two coffees over and Danie passed the joint. "So it's authentic."

"That's what you wanted," I said. "Right?"

"No. Yes. I don't know. It's just – the client. I've known him years, Ash. And he's into this stuff."

"So am I, or—"

"No. Not the way he is. I mean he actually gets off on it. That's not speculation, I know it for a fact. I saw his collection." Danie hunched over. "You think you know someone…"

"Fuck sake."

"It's all money, though. Right?"

"If it pays the bills," I said. It felt pretty sleazy to me as well.

"It'll do that all right."

Danie told me how much Chris (as I'll call him) was paying for the DVD, and how much he was willing to pay for the original film. I whistled, and remembered the old proverb about a fool and his money – or, in this case, a rampant sexual deviant. I try not to be judgemental, but I hope you'll agree that a) there's a line, and b) masturbating over headless children is definitely on the wrong side of it.

Danie drove me to Euston that afternoon. I felt oddly disappointed, as if I'd been used in one of the less enjoyable ways. I knew that was silly – she was busy, it had been a job of work, for which I'd been well-paid – and besides, she'd actually gone to bed with me, which was a pretty affectionate thing to do by any standards. Maybe that was the problem. The trip to London had felt like old times, a weekend away with an old friend and sometime lover, until suddenly it hadn't.

The riots had died down, but the sky darkened progressively as the train travelled North. In London, rain had been falling in a light drizzle; by Birmingham it was a downpour, and torrential by the time we reached Nottingham, where the train unexpectedly terminated. I stood shivering outside the station with the other passengers, waiting for a replacement bus due in half an hour, then an hour, then two, until the station staff finally admitted (from a safe distance) that it had been cancelled. It wasn't the first time that had happened, but at least on this occasion I could afford an overnight stay in a B&B instead of sleeping in the waiting room.

I got the rail replacement bus when it finally arrived the following afternoon. My phone had been out of commission since Kettering – no signal, no wi-fi – so I couldn't check my emails until I got home. When I did, there was a message from Danie, saying thanks for my help, it had been great to see me and did I fancy meeting up in Liverpool later that month? She had to collect the original film from the seller in person, and wasn't keen on doing so alone.

My mood immediately lightened and I emailed her a *yes* then and there, only realising afterward that I'd talked myself into working for free, but decided I didn't *really* mind.

By the time of the Liverpool trip, the trains were running more or less smoothly and the torrential rains had given way to a scorching, unseasonal heatwave. The train carriage had been boiling, and my own clothes hung off me, damp with sweat.

Danie met me outside Lime Street Station, once more wearing jeans and a black vest top, along with dark glasses for that woman-of-mystery air. Sun cream glistened on her shoulders. I think that was when I realised that part of me, at least, was still in love with her, and always would be.

"Fun trip down?" She offered one of the ice creams she was holding and I took it, glad of the cool moisture, even though it brought back memories of the headless children at Le Mans.

"Great," I lied. "So what's the plan?"

"I'll let you know when I find out," she said. "I'm still waiting for our friend to let us know. He sent a text earlier to say the Glasgow train's been delayed."

"There's a surprise."

Neither of us knew Liverpool well enough, so we caught a black cab from Lime Street to the Marriott on Queen Square. I made a show of reaching for my wallet but Danie waved me away. We weren't meeting the seller till later, thankfully: all I wanted just then was to take a long, cold shower and sprawl naked on the bed to dry off, ideally in Danie's company.

But she turned at the door to her room and put a hand on my chest, pointing to the room next door. "Easy, Tiger," she said. "You're in there."

She dropped my room key in my hand and shut her door in my face; by the time I'd let myself into my own double room, the shower next door was already hissing – indicating, at least, that great minds think alike.

The mind's a monkey, or so they say, but mine's more like a dog chasing its tail with more energy than brains. As I undressed for the shower I wondered if I'd said or done something to offend Danie during my last stay, or in my response or non-response to her emails. Of course, it might have nothing to do with me; perhaps Danie had met somebody else. That caused a pang of a different kind: as single friends, with or without benefits, we had each other, but couples tend to hang out with other couples. Or maybe she'd just decided the relationship was better kept strictly platonic, in which case, what kind of atrocious arsehole must I be for Danie to withdraw even that sign of favour?

Welcome to the inside of my head; no, I have no idea why I'm single either. I flopped onto the bed, half-naked, and said out loud: "This is not a healthy relationship." I knew it was true, and also that the knowledge would change nothing.

I stood back up, finished undressing and got into the shower. Once I'd dried off I laid out my best outfit, but didn't put it on as the room was still sweltering and I was already dripping sweat again.

My phone buzzed. A text from Danie: *Dinner at 7, Cote Brasserie.*

I lazed around and showered again before I began to dress; I was still lacing my boots when Danie tapped on the door. When I opened it, I saw she was wearing a midnight-blue sheath dress and Doc

Martens, the kind of outfit only she seemed able to pull off. It should have looked ridiculous, but didn't.

"You look great," I told her.

She looked me up and down. "You'll do. I suppose."

———

The seller's name was Heggie and he had a business website, but there was no photo of him on it, and no social media presence that we could find. We sat sipping chilled water (Danie) and cold beer (me) and wondering how we'd recognise him when he showed.

As it turned out, we had no need to worry; we'd been sitting at our table in the Brasserie for about half an hour when a wiry, bespectacled man in his fifties walked in. He wore jeans and a faded t-shirt. Perspiration was spreading out from under his arms. His brown hair hung to the nape of his neck, but the crown of his head was shiny and bald. It and his forehead glistened He spoke to one of the waiters, and I caught a hint of a Scottish accent. Then he strode over to our table, glancing from Danie to me, and said: "Miss Starmer?"

"Mr Heggie?" Danie offered a hand, but he'd already sat down and was wiping his face with a napkin. He smelt of sweat and stale tobacco. "Who's this?" he grunted, nodding at me.

"My associate, Mr Dhillon."

Heggie was now using the napkin to clean his grimy spectacle lenses. "And what's his game?"

"He's here to authenticate the footage," I said, pointedly.

"I thought you'd already done that."

"The DVD, yes, but—"

"Whatever." Heggie grabbed the menu. "I'll have a Nastro Azurro."

Danie pursed her lips and signalled a waiter – she's one of those annoying people who can summon them at will.

Heggie filled his glass carefully from the bottle, took a sip and sighed. "I needed that."

"So," said Danie. "The film?"

"Well, I haven't brought it with me. Do I look as though my head buttons up at the back?"

"No, I get that. But we do need to make sure it's the real thing."

Heggie sucked his teeth. They were yellow. "You've seen the DVD."

"Yes, and Mr Dhillon assures me the footage is authentic, otherwise we wouldn't be here." Mr Dhillon. Cool and formal. Was that why she'd put us in separate rooms, to make sure we both stayed professional? If so, maybe things would warm back up when the deal was done. The thought gave me a small, hopeful glow, and yes, I'm fully aware how pathetic that sounds. "But we want the original footage, not a duplicate."

"Look, hen," said Heggie, "You think I want to hang onto that thing? I'm not some bloody ghoul like you two."

I felt Danie stiffen beside me. "Not sure why you chose to sully your lily-white hands, then," she said. Shit. So much for keeping it cool and formal.

Heggie went red; one particularly angry crimson blotch was spreading across his bald pate. "Not that it's any of your business, but I need the money."

"Well, so do I," she said. "And I'm not bloody proud of it."

"I should damned well hope not," said Heggie. "It's nothing to be proud of."

"We're all in the same boat," I said. "None of us like the thing. We were hired to get it and none of us can afford to turn it down. I'm not exactly looking forward to watching it again either. We don't have to be mates, so let's just get this over with so we can all get paid. Yeah?"

Danie breathed out and jerked a thumb at me. "Yeah. What he said."

Heggie was still red, and his lips were pressed together, but finally he breathed out. "All right. All right. I'm sorry. I just…" A gesture. "This is not my normal line."

"It's not ours either, mate," said Danie. "Believe me."

"Fair enough."

"Right, then," said Danie. "Let's eat. I might not have mentioned this, but the client's covering wining and dining as a business expense. So I don't know about you two, but I'm having all three courses and something good off the wine list with coffee and liqueurs to follow." She winked at Heggie. "We'll just blame you and your expensive tastes."

Heggie burst out laughing, and the last of the ill feeling melted away. "Now you're talking my language, hen," he said, and reached for the menu.

"So what is it you normally do?" I asked him, over the starters.

"Old photographs and postcards, mostly," he said. "I grab them in bulk from car boots and charity shops and auctions and antique shops and what-have-you, and then I sort through and flog them – on eBay, mostly. It's not a bad living. Lot of people go for it. Happier, simpler times and all that." He shrugged. "It's not hard to see the appeal."

Neither of us could argue with that.

"Now and again there's other stuff – slides, you know, and once in a blue moon there's a reel of film. It's usually old home movies. All part of the nostalgia kick." He grinned, showing his yellow teeth again. "Couple of times it was old-fashioned porn."

"What, like a What The Butler Saw machine?"

"One was. The other one – well, as I said, there were a lot of home movies."

"On an old film camera?" said Danie.

"Aye. Nineteen-twenties, that was. German, I think – you know, the old Weimar Republic. Had a wee bit of a reputation for decadence."

"Sounds like your kind of thing, Ash," Danie grinned.

"Oi!"

"Anyway, that's about as near-the-knuckle as I get. I picked this stuff up as part of a job lot of gear when I was in the Lake District late earlier this year. Finally got round to setting up my old projector to watch it… well, you can imagine."

"Not what you were expecting?" I said.

"Fuck no. Fucking vile sight it was. I was tempted to burn it, I have to say."

Danie laughed. "That'd give our client a heart attack."

"And serve him bloody right," said Heggie. We clinked our glasses together on that sentiment. "So what about you two? What's your line?"

We told him, and he nodded along. "How long you two been together?"

"Together?" Danie actually went red. "Oh, we're not – I mean, we're just friends."

"Yeah," I said, hoping I didn't sound too horribly disappointed. "Just friends."

Heggie looked from one of us to the other, looked as though he was about to say something and then decided against it. "I could do with another beer," he said at last.

We worked our way through the mains, dessert, port and cheese and large amounts of strong black coffee, then finally called for the bill. "Shall we get to it, then?" said Heggie.

"Ready to do your thing, Ash?" said Danie.

She wasn't so bothered about getting me with a clear head this time, I noticed. But while I'd had several drinks, it had been over the course of a long and leisurely meal and I had no more than a light buzz. I didn't know if I'd have been considered safe to drive, but I certainly had no doubts about my ability to spot any fakery. Not that I anticipated any; I had no doubt that Heggie was on the level. "Ready when you are."

"Back to mine, then," Heggie said.

He obviously knew Liverpool better than either of us, and we followed him back to the Britannia Adelphi on Ranelagh Road, just off Copperas Hill. The walk and the night air chased the last of the alcohol buzz away, and by the time we got there I was stone cold sober.

Heggie had booked a third-floor twin room; Danie and I sat on the bed nearest the door while he set his projector up behind us and rigged up the screen by the curtained window, puffing on an e-cig all the while in reluctant deference to the hotel's non-smoking policy. It wasn't the size of a proper cinema screen, of course, but still several times larger than Danie's plasma TV, which meant that the Le Mans footage would be blown up larger than I'd ever watched it before. Joy of joys.

Heggie passed us the can containing the film itself. A yellowed piece of paper was taped to the side. On it, in faded, spidery writing, were the words *Le Mans – V Coldgrain, 1955*. Heggie worked quickly and efficiently, and took the can back off me when he was done; a minute or so later he said "All right, then," and switched off the lights.

The projector whirred and clattered; white light flared across the screen and onto the far wall. It contracted and tightened into a bright, regular rectangle as Heggie adjusted the projector. Numbers flashed across the screen, and then the footage was playing, in silence but for the clattering of the machine. Grains and flecks danced across the screen; flaws in the emulsion. The cars swerved past: Porsche, Maserati, Talbot, Jaguar.

And then there were the four that mattered: Hawthorn's D-Type Jag, Macklin's Austin Healey, and Levegh and Fangio's Mercedes SLRs. I heard Danie take a deep breath, felt the bed shift and knew she was looking away. That was fair enough. She had no wish to see what was coming next again, and there was no need for her to. That was my job.

Hawthorn pulled in and braked; Macklin swerved and braked in turn. Levegh made his hand signal to Fangio, and then his front wheel went up the back of the Austin Healey and...

The Mercedes tumbling, end over end; the impact, the explosion. The road surface flying past the camera. The wreck of the Mercedes. Levegh's burning corpse. And then we were among the dead and maimed once more. The camera's pitiless eye swept back and forth, recording.

Every second of footage was as it had been on the DVD: I'd watched it enough times by now to know it inside out. Everything was identical, except for one thing.

"What the hell's that?" I asked Heggie.

"What's what?"

"There. That a double exposure or what? None of that's on the DVD."

Light from the projector glinted off Heggie's spectacles. "I've no idea. It must be some sort of flaw in the emulsion, but I've no idea why it didn't transfer to the DVD as well."

"Flaw in the emulsion my shiny red arse," Danie said abruptly. "What the fuck?"

There were about a dozen transparent shapes in the frame. For the most part they were like ice or glass; you could tell they were there, but what was happening in the frame remained clearly visible through them.

They were vaguely humanoid, at least from the waist up. Below it, the body tapered and tattered away into a sort of loose, ragged tail. They had long, grasping arms, almost the length of their bodies, and their long, stretched-out heads rose from their shoulders directly without necks.

They were transparent, as I said – at first. Then, abruptly, they thickened and darkened to a dull, fuzzy grey, like thick smoke, and became fully visible. Their arms were outspread, the fingers grasping and ungrasping. Their heads were faceless, featureless, except for a pair of large, round pallid eyes that stared and occasionally blinked. Whatever they were, they hovered, their ragged tails dangling above the ground, over the bodies; the thickest concentration of them hung over the bodies of the children. Then they faded again, and it was barely possible to make them out.

"What the fuck is that?" I said. "That's not… what the hell is it?"

"I don't know," said Heggie. "I have no fucking clue, pal. That wasn't even there last time I looked."

"Eh?"

"It wasn't—"

But before he could say anything else, the grey shapes had solidified again, hovering over the dead and dying, those white, blind-looking eyes avid as they studied the carnage, blinking slowly. I had time to take in one further detail: the ragged tendrils their lower bodies dissolved into were in motion. They were writhing, reaching, and finally fastening on the bodies beneath them.

And then they looked up.

Their heads tilted upwards, so that they were staring directly at me – at *us*, but right then all I could feel was their scrutiny. If you can imagine having a light shone at you that was somehow bitterly cold – that was how it felt.

The eyes blinked slowly. I don't know why, but there was something truly horrible and disgusting about that. It had a slow, deliberate quality to it, as though they were studying and assessing me. Then one of them raised its long arm and pointed in my direction, and they moved forwards, those faces that weren't faces filling the screen.

"Shitting Christ!" I heard Heggie shout, and Danie let out a scream. The two of us scrambled backwards across the bed; I don't know which one of us knocked the projector, but it keeled over sideways to crash to the hotel room floor, and the picture went with it, slewing up from floor to ceiling in a grotesquely distorted shape – narrow at the floorward end and spread massively out across the top of the wall and the edge of the ceiling. The grey shapes had all swarmed into that part of the screen – the pictures of the crash's aftermath played out as normal below them, tilted on their side – and several blurred faces with pairs of huge, pale, blinking eyes stared down, their long-fingered hands appearing to paw at the surface of the screen from behind.

No way that could be possible, of course – whatever they were, they'd been caught on the film more than sixty years ago and must surely be far in the past – but in the seconds before Heggie pulled the plug out of the wall socket and the projector went dead they looked as though they were about to tear out of the screen in search of us.

"Fuck," said Danie from the floor behind the bed. "Fuck. Fuck. Fuck."

Heggie switched the room lights on. He was pale and shaking. With a grunted curse he stumbled to the projector and righted it, muttering and cooing over the machinery. He prised the reel loose and tossed it down on the bed. I suppose either Danie or I should have protested at the cavalier treatment of such a valuable piece of motorsport history (it would have sounded better than calling it 'snuff porn for our sick fuck of a client'), but we were too busy recoiling from it; neither of us wanted to be too close to the damned thing.

"Fuck," said Danie again, scooting back across the floor till she hit the far wall. She shut her eyes and took several breaths in and out. "All right," she said. "All right." She breathed out, opened her eyes, and pushed herself unsteadily to her feet. "Fuck."

"Jesus," said Heggie. "I've no idea what... Holy Christ, fucking bloody hell. Oh shite." And with that he ran to the ensuite bathroom with his hand over his mouth. I got off the bed and went over to Danie as I heard him being noisily sick. I reached out to touch her but she pulled away, shaking her head. "What did we just see?" she whispered. I just shook my head in return.

The toilet flushed; the taps in the bathroom ran. I heard Heggie gargle and spit. He emerged a moment later, rooted in a backpack that lay beside the bed, and pulled out half a bottle of Teacher's. "Who wants some?" he asked.

We both raised our hands.

"I've watched – let's see – tonight's the third time I'll have watched the film," he said. "The original one, I mean. First time I ran it through the projector to see what I had. Then again when I was transferring it to DVD, and now tonight. And I can tell you now, it did not fucking look like that."

He held the bottle out to me. I took it and passed it to Danie. I badly needed a nip too, but suspected her need was greater than mine. "Was there anything?" I said. "I mean anything weird?"

"Shadows," he said. "I remember when I first watched it there were shadows. Especially... when it got to the bodies. Sort of hovering over them. I'd no idea what it was. I suppose I thought the same as you, Mr Dhillon—"

"Ash, mate," I said, gratefully accepting the bottle off Danie as she finished with it. "I don't think we need to be formal after all this."

"Huh. Good point. Well, I'm Malcolm then. But aye, I thought the same as you did to begin with. Double exposure of some kind. Christ alone knows how, but – well, it wouldn't diminish the value of the footage. It's unique. Even without those things on it." He held out his hand for the Teacher's and took another long swallow. "The second time I saw it – I remember thinking the shadows were worse than I'd thought before. See, first time round I barely noticed them. They were there, aye, but it was nothing much. Second time around – well, as I say, I thought the problem must be worse than I'd first reckoned. Trick of the light last time, something like that. Well, what else was I going to think, that it'd changed all by itself?"

"Well it bloody did, didn't it?" said Danie.

"No fucking shit, hen. Sorry. I'm sorry. I'm just…"

"We all are," she said. "But it's not just the image getting stronger. It – I mean, you *saw*."

"*They* saw," I said, after a long pause. It needed saying, and neither Danie nor Heggie seemed willing to say it, not that there was any blaming them for that. "They saw us."

Danie was already shaking her head. "Come off it, Ash, that can't be right."

"You saw. We all did. They looked at us. They moved. They—"

"Don't!" She flinched away from me. We were silent for a while.

"They were trying to get out," said Heggie. "Weren't they?"

Danie hugged her knees and shook her head.

"I think they were," I said. "Yes."

"Can I have another go at that bottle?" said Danie. "Thanks. Jesus, that stuff's like petrol. Okay. So, never mind, for now, what we just saw or what it was. What do we *do* about it?"

"Burn the bloody thing?" suggested Heggie.

"What for?"

"Because it's… it's…"

"It's been ordered," said Danie, "and it's being paid for very handsomely. Enough to leave us all a lot better off. And by a man, who, let's not mince our words here, likes to crack one off over footage of headless kids. If whatever's on that film can get out, and they want to, try to, cause harm, then…"

"Then it couldn't happen to a nicer fella," said Heggie. "And, you know, we could always tell him the film's in a fragile condition. Shouldn't be watched often, or at all. I mean, he's got the DVD for watching. He'll still own the footage itself. So if he takes our advice, he should be fine."

"Should," I said. "We think."

"Well, I've not had any problems."

"Maybe you will, if you don't get rid of it sharpish," said Danie. "But let's say you're right. If he doesn't play the film itself, fine. If he does, and something happens, it's on his own head."

It still didn't feel right. None of us needed to say it, but we all felt there was genuine danger in that innocuous reel of film. Danie took a deep breath. "If we give it him, it's out of our hands and we should be able to forget about the whole bloody business. And if anything's going to happen – well, better him than us, right?"

She was sort of right, I thought – the client was the one with the predilection for this stuff, and it would only be a sort of justice if it came back to bite him. (*Caveat emptor*, indeed.) But at the same time, even then, there were misgivings – for me at least. I think maybe for Heggie, and I think even for Danie. We'd all played our part in this, giving him films of the mangled dead to drool over. There was a choice.

Heggie could have burned the film, but he hadn't. Danie could have turned down the work, but she hadn't. I could have ended my involvement with the confirmation that the footage was authentic – and right then, I could have been counselling what I think I already knew, deep down, to be the right course of action. What we all knew to be right – burn the film and tell Danie's friend Chris that it hadn't been the real deal, that it had been a cheap fake after all and nothing to interest him. It wasn't the greatest of choices, because God knew we all needed the money and we'd all feel the pain if we were without it – but a choice it still was.

And we made ours that night.

"Aye," said Heggie. "It serves the bugger right. That's what I say."

"Ash?" said Danie. There was something close to a plea in her eyes. *Tell me I'm right*, they were saying. *Tell me that this is a good thing to do.*

I do wonder sometimes what would have happened, how things might have gone, had I said no. Better, or worse? She might never have forgiven me. We might never have spoken again, but we might have been spared what followed. Or not. Who's to say? God, even now I rationalise. I don't know if it was for her or out of my own need for her, out of the need for the money, maybe even out of some sort of curiosity, to see what might happen if we passed the film on to Chris. God help me, I even – *we* even – felt righteous about it. Poetic justice. Serves him right. But it had nothing to do with justice, and everything to do with selfishness and greed. And with whatever I felt for Danie.

And in the end, none of that matters; it only matters what I didn't say, and what I did.

"Yes," I told them both. "It serves the bugger right."

———

Heggie packed his gear away, and Danie called Chris' number to confirm the footage was authentic, if fragile. Chris *umm*ed and *ahh*ed, but agreed the terms. After all, he could watch the DVD to his heart's content, over and over again. Just to *have* the original footage would be enough.

Funds were transferred; there was some holding of breath around this point as the online banking system had been affected by some recent cyber-attacks, not to mention the brown-outs that had hit the north-west along with various other regions in recent months. It took nearly an hour – a tense one, during which the bottle of Teacher's was diminished still further – before Heggie checked his account and found his balance pleasantly improved. At which point, he handed over the reel, wrapped in plastic and sealed into a padded envelope, shook hands with us both and offered a final nip of the bottle before bidding us goodnight.

Danie and I stepped briefly outside the hotel into the night air that once again, hot and muggy though it was, seemed to sober me up almost at once. It was a noisy night. Drunks were staggering along Copperas Hill, someone was screaming something at someone else – so high-pitched, weepy and hysterical it was impossible to tell the sex – and being answered with cruel laughter. Another voice was furiously bellowing obscenities and threats, and there was a sound of breaking glass.

"Cab?" I suggested.

"Too bloody right," said Danie, taking out her phone, then grinned and gave me a quick one-armed hug. "We can afford it."

The *We* and the feeling the hug gave me warmed me far more than it should.

The cab took us back to the Marriott, where Danie had the envelope containing the reel put into the hotel safe. We took the lift up again; we had it to ourselves and I was suddenly aware of the warmth of her body under that dress.

"You okay?" she asked. Sweat glistened at her throat, on the upper slopes of her breasts. I looked away.

"Yeah. Just a bit tired." I could have kicked myself for that. "Nothing a coffee won't fix."

"Mm." The lift chimed and the doors opened. "Think I've had enough excitement for one night. I'm gonna turn in."

"Right." We'd reached her room. I stood there awkwardly for a moment. "Okay," I said, trying to think of what to say next; what, if anything, she wanted to hear.

"Night, Ash," she said, and a moment later the door clicked shut in my face again. I sighed, and went on to my room. Next door, the shower hissed. I undressed and wandered into the bathroom, turning on and stepping under the hot spray as well. I felt grimy, as much from the evening's business as from the heat and sweat.

I dried off and was about to climb into bed when there was a tap at the door. I grabbed a fluffy towelling robe and answered it. Danie stood there, hair still hanging in damp ringlets, wearing only a t-shirt that hung almost to her knees.

"I'd rather not sleep alone," she said at last.

I nodded. "To be honest, neither would I."

"No sex," she said. "Not tonight. Is that okay?"

"Okay."

"I just want to be held."

"I can do that."

"Okay, then," she said, and I held the door wide.

When I woke up in the morning, she'd already gone, leaving a brief note that she was catching an early breakfast before heading back to London. I think I dressed more quickly than I had in years, and hurried downstairs.

She sat alone at a table by the window, wearing dark glasses, and sighed when I came to join her. "What do you want?" she said.

That hurt. "Well, just to have breakfast with you before you go."

Another sigh. "Fine."

I suppose I should have taken the hint and gone away, but having to find a table by myself and eat alone would somehow have been even more humiliating, so I didn't.

Danie ate, scrolling through news articles on her tablet. "Glad it's over," I said at last.

"What?" she said irritably, looking up.

"The… whole business with the film," I said, rather lamely. I think if a kicked dog could have spoken, it would have sounded like me then.

"Yes," she said, pointedly. "It's over."

I took the hint and didn't say anything else. I ate my breakfast as quickly as I could, but it wasn't easy: it tasted of nothing and stuck in my throat. Danie nibbled toast and sipped black coffee throughout, scrolling on through her tablet, as though I wasn't there. In the end I left my breakfast unfinished, went back up, took one last shower and packed everything away. I peeped into the dining area when I came back down to check out, but she'd gone.

My wi-fi access went all to hell again on the journey home, but when I finally could access my emails there was one from her, apologising for being short with me. She blamed the hangover, the horrible weirdness of the footage, and the client, the whole nature of the job. *Speak soon*, she added at the end, *The D xxx*.

That sign-off filled me with a strange blend of nostalgia, warmth and cynical irritation. *The D* had been my nickname for her at University. It hadn't really caught on with anyone else; it had just been me trying to sound cool and in particular as though I didn't give a toss about her charms. It hadn't convinced anyone then either. God, I was contemptible. Even more so because I knew she was using the nickname deliberately to make me feel better about how we'd left things in Liverpool, so that she'd be able to get the old horse out of the stable again the next time she needed me, and because I knew that it would work.

I did my best to forget about Danie. Even though I was comfortably off after the job and could have taken more time for myself – a holiday maybe – I threw myself into new work. To be fair, a holiday would probably have been more stressful than not going anywhere, given the state of public transport, the wildfires in Scotland and the Lake District and the Byzantine process of arranging travel outside the UK, but even so, it wasn't the distraction I needed. Being alone with my thoughts was not appealing.

Much of it was Danie, of course. I did go on a few dates – internet access, while patchy in the wake of the latest brownouts and a week of bad electrical storms, worked well enough to arrange a few hookups. But I soon realised I was picking women based on their resemblance to Danie; the sex, when it happened, was generally fine, but things never went further because they weren't her. After that, I made a point of picking women who resembled Danie as little as possible, and that was disastrous on the physical front as well as every other.

I may have hated her a little by that point, for sleeping with me in London. It had reawakened a whole catalogue of things I'd thought long dead. I was not over Danie, and never had been. Pathetic? Yes, I was; I am. I freely admit it. I didn't want to be, but I had no idea how to break out of the trap. Except through work. And, yes, by dating women who reminded me of her. Hookups weren't hard to come by: I was still reasonably presentable, could manage a decent conversation when required, and I could perform at least adequately in bed. Danie had taught me well.

So much in my life, I realised, for good and ill, could be traced back to her. If I'd believed in soulmates, I might have considered her mine – only with the added complication, thanks to a universe with a cruel sense of irony, that our respective temperaments made living together impossible.

I swung between wanting to plead with her for some sort of ongoing relationship, on whatever terms she wanted, and trying to find a way to break with her altogether and move on to someone new. Of course, since I didn't hear from her after Liverpool, other than that one email, and could think of no pretext on which to contact her again (other than to bluntly declare my feelings, which knowing Danie would have her pulling the shutters down at speed), I couldn't do either.

So I worked, I hooked up, and when I couldn't manage that I masturbated with a mixture of frustrated lust, anger and self-loathing. I ate junk food and shut myself in; I went on a health kick and ate salads and went for runs. None of it really helped.

But at least the business of the Le Mans footage was behind me, except for one incident that I did my best to dismiss as a dream, a hallucination, a last psychic echo of the more disturbing aspects of the whole affair.

One night, or more correctly in the very early hours of one morning, about a fortnight after our meeting with Heggie, I was suddenly awake in bed. It was a very sharp transition from sleep to consciousness, strangely so as I'd gone to bed very late after a long day: I could only have been asleep for two or three hours, so there was no way I could describe myself as being well-rested.

I was lying in a foetal position. That in itself wasn't particularly unusual, but I was unable to move. And then, after a second or so of this, I felt the bed behind me shift, as though someone had sat on the edge of it. I suppose I should add at this point that I was alone in my house: I occasionally came back here with women I hooked up with (although quite rarely, since driving out to a cottage in the middle of nowhere with a man they hardly knew didn't usually give women the sense of security they preferred when dating; it was more common to meet for a drink in Sheffield, then go to a hotel), but not that night. So there should have been nobody there to sit upon the bed.

I wanted to turn over, but for nearly a minute I was incapable of moving – and, in addition, I was frightened of what I might see if I did. But eventually the paralysis broke, and I rolled over: the fright I felt escalated to even higher levels in the instant before the side of the bed came in sight. Then it dropped somewhat, as there was, of course, no one there.

This wasn't a unique experience for me; it had happened a couple of times in the past. Sleep paralysis; it's not uncommon, and often goes with the phenomenon of 'felt presences', which are considered to be a psychological rather than supernatural occurrence. To be honest, I'm still not certain if this wasn't just another instance of the same thing. It's only subsequent events that make me wonder otherwise.

As had happened on the previous occasions, I switched the bedside light on – there was another little peak of terror there, where I was convinced the light would disclose something horrible, but it didn't – and sat up, knowing that it would be some time, if at all, before I'd be able to get back to sleep that night.

I badly needed to pee, but the dread that normally accompanied these episodes was still oppressively present; it wasn't so bad in the lit room (although the slightest sound, or shadow in my peripheral vision, was still enough to make me start) but the thought of the unknown dark outside the door sent it ratcheting up. I knew, of course, that there was nothing unknown there – it was just my old familiar hallway – but fear is rarely a rational emotion.

I did what I usually did in such circumstances: I picked up the book on my bedside table (there's always one there) and started to read. Experience tended to show that the anxiety very quickly faded away when I did this.

On this occasion, though, it didn't. If anything, it intensified, and the sense of something dark and unknown and hostile surrounding the room and pressing in on me from all sides built up to the point where I thought I heard the walls and ceiling creak under the pressure of it. When I listened more intently, there was only a silence so complete that I wished I had a CD player in the room.

Ideally I'd have preferred to sit up reading until it became light outside, or until I was tired enough to drift off (with the light on, obviously.) Unfortunately, my bladder had other ideas.

I did my best to ignore it, but in the end, it was impossible. So I reluctantly climbed out of bed and made for the bedroom door. I don't think I ever wished so fervently for an ensuite bathroom as I did then.

I pulled the door open in roughly the same way you rip off a Band-aid: to get through the suffering quickly and before I could think about it. The fear that there'd be something behind it had risen to a conviction by that point, but the hallway was empty except for the greyish, soupy dark.

I stepped out into the hall and started for the bathroom. The dark was a grey haze, a bit like static on a television screen, blurring the outlines of everything in the hall to the point that they almost, but not quite, melted into one another. And then it stirred.

It was a vague shape, very tall and narrow. It didn't really look at all humanoid – not at first – more like an elongated cylinder floating in the air. As it became more distinct I saw that the lower end hovered about six inches above the hall carpet and the upper end was about the same distance short of the ceiling. Which would make it about nine feet tall.

As it moved, it became more distinct. The lower end became tapered and tattered. So did the top end, putting me in mind of a pointed hood. And then the middle of it writhed, and unfolded into a pair of very thin, very long arms, ending in equally long thin hands. Up until then the shape's presence had been accompanied by a thick, preternatural silence, so blanketing that even the clock I kept on the living-room mantelpiece, whose ticking I could sometimes hear even in my bedroom with the door shut, was inaudible, but now I was sure I heard a soft whispering sound as those limbs brushed against the wall: the shape seemed to be trying to spread its arms out, but the hall was too narrow.

By then, of course, I knew exactly what I was looking at, and the vision could have disappeared then and there and ensured me a sleepless remainder of the night, but it wasn't done with me. Two further things happened. One was that two large, round eyes, whitish, lit with a kind of vague dull phosphorescent light, opened in that pointed head and slowly, deliberately blinked. The second was that those long hands groped – blindly, it seemed, at first – along the walls, and then reached out towards me.

I made some sort of sound; I'm not quite sure what. And then, despite the apparition in front of me, my attention shifted to a sensation of hot liquid coursing down my legs. I experienced a second of shame and self-disgust, and fear of another kind – I was clinging, in that second, to the idea that I was hallucinating the shape and that it, together with the sudden loss of bladder control, suggested some sort of neurological dysfunction. It only lasted for a second, as I've said, and then I looked up.

If I'd known an instant of hope that the thing would be gone, the illusion dispelled, it vanished as soon as I looked up: the groping hands had advanced along the walls, towing their owner after them, and were now embedded in the wallpaper – the tips of the fingers, I registered, looked very curved and sharp – on either side of my head. The thing's pale round eyes blinked again as it neared me, and the fingers pulled free of the wall and swept in towards my head.

I made another sort of sound, and if my bladder hadn't been empty it would have given way a second time. I blundered backwards, collided with the small table that the old – almost never-used – landline telephone rested on, and then both it and I crashed to the ground. Above me the hazy dark writhed and moved: I couldn't see those blank, whitish eyes, but knew they'd appear at any moment, and that when they did those groping hands would follow. I wasn't sure what would happen if they fastened on me; I only knew that they mustn't, not at any cost.

I fumbled across the floor, and found the table lamp that had stood on the table beside the phone. I snatched it up, and as the white, blinking eyes showed above me I switched it on and thrust it forward and up.

Light spilled across the hallway, and it was empty. I was by myself, sprawled on my back with the leggings I wore to bed soaking wet. The shape was gone.

I switched on every light in the house, changed into dry clothes, threw the wet ones into the washing machine, drank strong coffee until it was light and did my best to convince myself that nothing had ever been there.

———

Early one morning three days later, Danie called me again.

"Ash?" she said. "Are you okay?"

"Well, I'm here, aren't I?" I said.

"Seriously?"

"Yeah. Yeah, I'm okay. You? What's wrong?"

"It's Heggie," she told me.

"What about him?"

She hesitated. "You hadn't heard from him or anything? He'd not been in touch, or…"

"No. No. I mean, why would he? Danie, what is it?"

"He's dead," she told me. "He killed himself."

———

The internet was having a good day, so we agreed to try a video-call. Danie was upset – weirdly so. She isn't cold-blooded and ruthless – well, not completely;

as I said before, there's a reason she's more successful than me – but she isn't what you'd call overemotional at the best of times. And being a woman running her own business in what could be a pretty tough market made her even less prone to emotional displays. I'd seen her show far less in response to the deaths of people she'd known far better than Heggie.

We'd met the guy once, after all, and while we'd ended up getting on well enough I didn't think we'd be sending one another birthday or Christmas cards (despite the name, I was raised a Christian, however nominally), far less dinner invites. We had one thing in common, and it was something we'd wanted to put behind us and forget; not exactly a basis for a long-term friendship.

But here Danie was in a rumpled black vest top, with no make-up, galloping bed-hair and a general air of very little sleep. She was smoking, and I guessed from the haziness of the air around her that it wasn't her first cigarette of the day.

"Fuck me," I said. "Are you okay?"

"No." She shook her head. "No, I don't think I am at all."

"Why? What exactly happened?"

"Well, I told you. Heggie."

"Well, yeah, but…" I trailed off. Obviously neither of us had known Heggie that well, and it was entirely possible there'd been a host of other issues bedevilling him that we'd known nothing about, but the timing of his death – after what the three of us had witnessed, as well as my experience of a few nights before – made that difficult to believe. "How did you find out?"

"The police," she said. "You'll probably hear from them before long. I was the last person he'd spoken to – well, we were. There were other names in his diary, but he hadn't seen them. He hadn't seen anyone since…"

"Since he met us."

She nodded.

Neither of us spoke right after that. Danie lit a fresh cigarette with the one she'd been puffing on and took a very long drag.

"Careful," I said, "you'll gas yourself."

"Fuck off."

I opened my mouth to speak, but as I did, my doorbell rang.

"I think that's the rozzers," I said. Danie managed a wan smile at the expression. "I'll call you back, okay?"

She nodded. "Please," she said. I couldn't be certain because the picture resolution wasn't great (and there was the smoke to consider) but I think there were tears in her eyes.

———

I placed another video call to her about an hour and a half later, once the police car was out of sight and I'd brewed a pot of very strong tea. We all have our different ways of coping. While I like a drink, alcohol had been a strict no-no in our household when I was growing up. But my strictly teetotal parents both always had an almost mystical faith in the power of tea, stewed to creosote strength, with a tiny amount of milk and what at times tasted like half a kilo bag of sugar, as a restorative in the face of all trauma. I'm pretty sure that if The Bomb had dropped and we'd all been crawling around screaming with our faces burned off and the first symptoms of fatal radiation sickness emerging, Mum's first objective would have been to find a way to boil the kettle. Anyway, it's a taste I immediately associate with comfort, with bad things fading into the background, and normal service generally being resumed. Once I'd poured myself a mug of the stuff, I called Danie and we compared notes.

Heggie had thrown himself from an upstairs window of his house. The impact had injured him badly, perhaps even fatally, but he might have survived if the ambulance had got there in time. He was still conscious, however, and carrying a knife, and one of his arms had been unbroken. He'd stabbed himself about a dozen times in the chest and stomach, finally snapping the blade, before cutting his throat with the jagged stump of it. He'd taken a couple of minutes to bleed out. Cold, lonely and painful ones, the young and rather sinister detective constable who'd come to my door had informed me, taking a pretty ghoulish relish in doing so.

The police officer Danie had dealt with had been less of a gorehound and more sympathetic. Detective Constable Al-Ghul had remembered to ask me if I knew of anyone who'd wish Heggie ill or if he'd seemed afraid when we met him. He hadn't gone into detail about the state of Heggie's house, but Danie's interrogator had.

As far as his neighbours and few acquaintances could tell, Heggie hadn't left his home since returning from Liverpool. They'd reported all the lights being on at all hours – at first, at least. That might have been why all the bulbs had blown out. He'd spent much of his time in his bedroom with a stock of tinned and dried food and a hotplate – there was an ensuite bathroom for water and sanitation. It looked as though his suicide had followed the final bulb blowing out in the middle of the night.

"He didn't seem afraid of the dark when we met him," I said at last, once Danie had finished speaking. It was an attempt at humour that fell flat and dull between us, like the crushed remains of something small and dead.

"Have you…" she hesitated. "Seen anything? Since then?"

I thought of my experience of three nights before. "No," I lied. "You?"

She shook her head. "No," she said. "No."

I knew she was lying too. And she knew I was; of course she did.

"Do you think it's anything to do with…" she began, and let the sentence hang.

"What do you think?" I said.

We weren't expecting to hear from the police again. There'd been rioting in Sheffield, the aftermath of which was tying up most of their personnel. 'Protest marches' by far-right groups in response to several incidents of knife crime (no proof, in most cases, that the criminals had been non-white or Muslim, but the people behind the chaos regarded facts as a superfluous detail at best) had turned violent; given that Molotov cocktails and various hand weapons had been quickly deployed, it seemed likely that had been the intention all along. Windows had been smashed, houses firebombed, people beaten up and – ironically, I suppose you could say – there'd been two fatal stabbings. At times like this I was even more grateful than usual for my quiet little place in the hills.

Some of the angry young men in the Muslim community had retaliated, either going after meeting-places for the groups that had orchestrated the whole affair or – more worryingly – venturing into areas with a predominantly white population to throw bricks or – even more worryingly – petrol bombs of their own. Between trying to contain the situation and hunting down the main offenders for arrest and trial (the far-right organisers, having planned it all along, had mostly vanished into hiding, so most of the major arrests in the aftermath were of young Asian men, which helped stoke the fires too), both uniformed and CID officers had far higher priorities than assisting Police Scotland with what was, after all, a suicide, albeit a bizarre one. And in London, the Met – reeling from yet another round of cuts – was just as overworked.

The police on Heggie's own patch weren't likely to find anything either, if he'd been afraid of what I thought. Not that they knew anything about it. Neither Danie nor I had mentioned the film's 'hidden extras' to them. Apart from that, though, I'd hidden nothing. What was there to hide? We hadn't done anything illegal: unethical and disgusting maybe, given why 'Chris' had wanted the footage, (although now I think of it, neither of us told the police *that*, either), but ultimately all we'd done was buy a reel of film. Heggie had been paid, everyone had got what they wanted, and our client could readily spare the cash he'd forked out.

Danie had withheld her client's identity pending contact with him, but gave the police his solicitor's details (a big firm with hundreds of wealthy clients) before emailing 'Chris' to let him know what had happened. Just then I think she was more frightened of 'Chris' than of the things on the film – I doubt she really believed he'd had anything to do with Heggie's death, but she certainly didn't think him incapable of that kind of thing, and had no desire to anger him. Luckily he took it well – it helped that she hadn't told the police why he'd wanted the film in the first place ("He's very interested in the history of motorsport") – and was getting in touch with his solicitors to arrange damage limitation.

Danie has a few police connections, so we were able to add to what we knew within two hours of the visits. Danie had briefly wondered if 'Chris', either out of a belief that he'd been overcharged or plain stinginess (you don't become a millionaire through sweetness of character and unbridled generosity, after all,) might have decided to get his money back, but there was no doubt that Heggie's injuries had been self-inflicted.

Admittedly, suicides tended to open the window before jumping, but Heggie's house had yielded no evidence of forced entry, or even anyone else's presence in it for months before. And they found the money Danie had given Heggie. The envelope had been opened, but only a couple of notes were missing. They found them in the toilet; he'd run out of paper.

I learned all this during the my second video-call of the day with Danie. She looked less frazzled, having showered and dressed, but was still shaken and afraid. "So *now* what?" she said.

I didn't answer at first. I didn't ask again if she'd experienced anything weird recently: I baulked whenever I thought of describing what had happened to me. Some of that was the fear of how ridiculous it would sound, but there was another fear – deeper and more primitive – that if I spoke about what I'd seen, I might call its attention back to me.

"Well, the police aren't going to investigate what was on the film," I said at last.

"They can't. We didn't tell them." Danie snorted. "And they wouldn't have believed us if we did."

"No. But there's nothing to stop us doing a little quiet digging of our own, is there?"

"Do you think…" Danie licked her lips. "Do you think that's a good idea?"

"Do you think it's a good idea to sit around and wait to see what happens next?"

She breathed out. "All right. So where do we start?"

<hr />

We compared notes. Heggie had told us he'd picked up the reel from an antique shop in the Lakes, part of a job lot of material. "That's our first lead," said Danie. "See if we can find out who all this shit belonged to."

"Coldgrain," I said.

"Say what now?"

I'd been trying to remember the name for the past few minutes. "The film can," I said, "with the footage on. There was a name on it. I've been trying to remember what it was, all I could remember was that it was a pretty unusual one. Coldgrain. C-O-L-D-G-R-A-I-N. That was it. V. Coldgrain."

"Good. That narrows it down." Danie breathed out. "Okay, look. I'll get in touch with my police contacts, see if I can get a shufti at Heggie's accounts."

"You can pull that off?"

"I've a few favours I can call in. Don't ask."

She wouldn't meet my eyes when she said that. Up until then I'd believed – maybe because I wanted to – that Danie's career had been as above-board and morally irreproachable as it was possible to be in the media. Wishful thinking, I know. Now, though – well, I followed her advice and I didn't ask.

"You wanna see what you can dig up about this Coldgrain bloke?" she said.

"Okay."

"Thanks, Ash." She reached out and rested her hand against the screen. "Seriously."

I reached out and laid my hand against the screen as well, over hers. "Any time," I said, and the saddest thing of all was that I knew I meant it.

A few online searches threw up what little there was to be found about *V Coldgrain* – Victor Coldgrain, as it turned out.

His name first popped up on the IMDb in connection with old British silent movies in the 1920s. He'd been director of photography on an early Hitchcock film, and on any number of productions by less illustrious directors. In the 1930s his name cropped up in connection with a dozen or so Hollywood B-movies, the last one in early 1939. After that – nothing.

So he'd either died or retired from the movies at that point. If he'd died, then a different *V Coldgrain* must have shot the Le Mans footage (unless he'd risen from the grave to film it, which I wasn't quite ready to entertain at that stage.) If he'd retired, what had he done? Worked for the newsreels, perhaps?

I fired off a couple of emails to two of my more knowledgeable friends. Paddy Meehan knew more about the movies than I'd thought it possible to know before I met her, and Tony Hagopian was an expert on old newsreel firms like Pathé, Gaumont, Empire, and Movietone.

Another email arrived just after I'd sent one to Tony. That was quick, I thought, then saw it was from Danie. *Success*, it read. *Spk in a bit*.

I drummed my fingers on the desktop. Now I wanted to email her back with something of my own, but there was so little. No. I wanted to impress her – the same humiliating need for her approval, the hope of being tossed a bone – and that meant waiting till I (hopefully) had more.

It was getting dark outside, close to dusk – but I went out for a run anyway. I knew the track that led around the moorland near the cottage pretty well, and there was something about the twilight I enjoyed, especially with the tiny lights of Sheffield glimmering nearby.

There normally was, anyway. The dim light and the resulting loss of definition in the landscape was unpleasantly reminiscent of the darkened hallway the other night. Years before, back at University – and yes, before you ask, it had been in the company and at the urging of Danie – I'd taken LSD; I'd spent a lot of the time grinning like a complete pillock and finding utter fascination in very ordinary objects, but a couple of times I'd seen things shift, suddenly change shape and form. Only for a moment, but in each case I'd kept staring for ages afterwards, hoping I'd see it again. I hadn't, but there'd been a number of times where some ordinary household item had seemed charged with a kind of weird potential, as though at any moment it might shift too. I was reminded of that experience, too, on my run, and not at all pleasantly. The hazy dark seemed constantly threatening to resolve itself into a hovering, long-armed shape with pallid, slowly-blinking eyes. When the rain intensified and started to include hailstones, I cut the run short and headed home.

All the lights were on, a habit I'd got into since my encounter in the hallway – it helped my peace of mind a little, if not my bank balance when the bill came in. I locked the door behind me and returned to the laptop to find emails waiting from both Paddy and Tony.

Tony's was first, and the driest: he's a lovely bloke, when you can actually coax him out into the daylight, but he spends most of his time among his files and archives and rarely ventures forth. Victor Coldgrain had worked briefly for several of the lesser-known newsreel firms in the late 1940s and early to mid '50s. He seemed to have dropped off the map around the end of 1954 – that, at least, was the last reference Tony had found for him. *Hope that helps*, he said, *Wishes, Tony*.

Well, at least it potentially put Coldgrain at Le Mans on the day. But that was superfluous: it wasn't as though there were any doubts about the reel's authenticity. By this point, I'd have been quite happy if there had been and I could prove the whole thing some kind of macabre and insanely complicated hoax, perhaps including the film stock being imbued with some sort of psychotropic that was making us all hallucinate (shades of University once more, not to mention desperation.)

Paddy's message said simply *Hullo! Drop us a Skype why don't ya. P xxx.* She and Tony are very different people. Paddy and I go way back – all the way back to Hull University, in fact, where she was on the same course as Danie and I. She'd ended up combining her love of history with her love of cinema, had gone on to take a second degree in Film Studies and was hugely in demand as a movie historian, especially when it came the British film industry. After giving myself a quick once-over in the mirror to make sure my appearance wouldn't frighten a police horse, I placed a video-call to her.

Paddy's thin, sharp features sprang into view. "Ashy! Long time no see. How've yous been? What's the crack?"

"I'm good," I lied.

"It's Ash," Paddy called. Her girlfriend Mary popped up in the background and waved, their daughter Annie in tow. "Hey, Ash. You okay? Say hi to Uncle Ash, Annie."

"Hiya, Uncle Ash."

"Hi Annie. Hi Mary. Yeah, I'm all right."

"Be with you in a minute, babe," said Paddy, and after a few quick farewells the door clicked shut behind Mary and Annie. "Right," she said, taking a gulp from a large mug of tea. "Victor Coldgrain, you were asking about."

"Yeah."

"All right. Pretty grim tale, to be honest with you. Well, sad, rather than grim. He was good at his job – could have gone a long way – but shit went wrong for him, as it so often does. God knows I love my fillums—" Paddy always said 'fillum' rather than 'film'; I was never sure if that was a genuine quirk of pronunciation or whether she'd started saying it as a joke and now couldn't stop herself "—but I'm glad I just write about them instead of working on them. What do you know so far?"

I told her. Paddy sucked her teeth. "Just what's on the IMDb, then. Half the story as ever, if that. All right, then. So he was born into a theatre family in London, 1899. Mother used to be an actress, turned wardrobe mistress. Dad was a stage manager and photographer. Did publicity stills for productions, that sort of thing. Rumour hath it he did other kinds of photos too, sometimes using the costumes his wife knocked out – but that's nothing to do with the story. Just a wee tidbit to warm your cockles. Anyway."

Young Victor had developed an interest in both showbiz and photography; like his father, his talents lay on the technical side of things, and he'd assisted him in his work. Even Paddy wasn't sure of the details of how he'd transitioned from still photography to the moving image, but that had been underway shortly after the end of the First World War. A need to earn a more substantial crust may have come into it, as one thing she *did* know was that both of his parents had died in the Spanish flu pandemic that had swept across the world in the last months of the war and the first year of the uneasy peace.

"He was a bright young fella," Paddy said. "Enthusiastic and good at his job. Worked his way up PDQ from being an assistant this and that to cinematographer on a whole bunch of early silents with half the major directors of the time – W.P, Kellino, Maurice Elvey, Kenelm Foss. IMDB doesn't have the half of it, like I said – well, Jesus, you know how many fillums have been lost over the years, Ash…"

I nodded. That was one of Paddy's favourite hobby-horses. Another time I might have tried to steer her back on topic, but a) there was no knowing what tiny detail might prove of use and b) any distraction from current affairs was welcome.

"Anyway," said Paddy at last, following rundowns on several of the lost films Coldgrain had worked on, and a short disquisition on others of the period that he hadn't but which she still deemed significant, "he made the jump to talkies and by 1930 he had his eye on America. The Great Depression was on by then, and he had a family too. Wife and a wee boy. I'll come back to them. But anyway, he emigrated there to work in Tinseltown because by God, if there was one industry still going full-tilt there it was the old dream factory. As I say, he was a good DP – God, stop sniggering, Ash, you know you watch way too much porn for your own good, it'll stunt your growth and you'll go blind – so he didn't find himself short of work. I mean, no particular classics that I can name, although there's a rumour or three he did a wee bit of uncredited work on *Scarface* and *Public Enemy*. But he made a good living. They were good years for him. But come 1939, he did a David Niven."

"Huh?"

"Niven! The boy had a grand Hollywood career going for him, but when the war kicked off he dropped everything and ran back home to enlist. Well, Coldgrain was nowhere near as big a name, but he did the same thing. They turned him down, though – he was pushing the limit for military age, though God knew they needed the bodies just then –

but he'd never exactly been a prime physical specimen, and besides, the powers that be decided he'd be put to better use elsewhere."

"Propaganda films?"

"Propaganda fillums, instructional stuff, and as things went on, a good few of those stiff-upper-lip there'll-always-be-an-England let-us-stand-strong-against-the-evil-Huns type dramas. Again, nothing particularly exalted, but he kept himself busy and he did his part, as they say. So. So far, so fairly unexceptional, right?"

I nodded. "So what changed?" I knew Paddy and how she liked to tell a story well enough by now.

"His family, that's what. I said I'd come back to them, did I not? Now let's just twizzle the rewind button and go back to 1920. Your man Coldgrain, he's no family at that time – the Spanish flu, remember? Now I don't know if you knew this already but after the Great War there was a *massive* wave of interest in spiritualism – what with the War and the flu pandemic there were that many people who'd lost loved ones and they wanted… well, they wanted answers, and more than that they wanted to see their loved ones again, or at least know that they weren't gone for good. That they'd meet again on the other side – well, you can hardly blame folk for that, can you?"

"No," I agreed.

"Aye, well – young Victor Coldgrain, he's reeling from losing his parents, so of course he attends his share of séances and table-tappings. The appeal soon wears off, but not before he meets a pretty young war widow by the name of Sybil Gowland. She's the better part of ten years older than him—" Paddy hummed a couple of bars of 'Mrs Robinson' "—but they fall into bed together. They're both alone in the world, they both need someone, so, there you have it. So they get married, and in June of 1921 a son and heir comes along – Julian Coldgrain, apple of his parents' eyes. Sybil'd been married before but there'd been no weans – everyone assumed *her womb was barren*, but it looked as though Mr Gowland might have been a Jaffa instead."

"A *what?*"

Paddy rolled her eyes. "Seedless."

"Parenthood obviously agrees with you. You're churning out the Dad jokes now."

She raised a middle finger. "You want my help or not, you cheeky arse?"

"Sorry."

Paddy grinned. "So they've a wee boy, raised in London and LA. Good-looking young man – if you check your inbox in five minutes' time I'll email some family photos over to you – and patriotic with it. You know how it is for some folk – give them a home country they haven't set foot in for years, and they go mad for it. Or one they've never been to in their lives, but they had a granny from there…"

"Are you going to go off on one about St Patrick's Day again?"

"It's a bastarding disgrace the way it gets co-opted by yous Brits and the Yanks. Cultural fucking appropriation, that's what it is. But anyway. Young Master Coldgrain, he's the patriotic type. Probably helps that he did a lot of his growing up in LA and not London – not quite as many memories of all the poor bastards who'd come back from the Western Front minus limbs, eyes, faces or sanity. But anyway, they've barely been home five minutes before out he trots, straight down to the recruiting office, lies about his age and joins up. Cue much blood and thunder from Victor, attacks of the vapours and clutching of pearls from Sybil."

Paddy sighed, and the air went out of her. "Anyway," she said. "Long story short. Fast forward to 1942, and Corporal Julian Coldgrain's among the men from 3 Commando assigned to take part in Operation Jubilee."

"Which was…?"

"The Dieppe Raid. First attempt since Dunkirk to take on the Wehrmacht in Occupied France. The idea was to hold the port for a short period to show that it could be done, and that the Allies could and would open a western front in Europe. Didn't go well. They never got off the beach. Lot of young men never made it home again from that."

"And Julian Coldgrain was one of them?"

Paddy shook her head. "Might have been better if he had been, though. The doctors were pretty amazed he'd pulled through at all. Third-degree burns, bullet and shrapnel wounds. He lost an eye, both arms and a leg, half his innards I think and his face – well, you'll see. I'll email you."

"No need—"

"It's no bother."

I shook my head in sheer awe. "How the hell did you get all this information?"

"It's what I *do*, Ashy. So he lived. For a time. Died in early '45. Broke his parents, seeing him like that. But he still outlived his mother. Sybil Coldgrain was out food shopping one fine day in '44, when a V-2 blew up the street. Killed outright."

"God."

"That's war. So, when the dust settles, Coldgrain's come through another war but once again he's alone in the world. Unsurprisingly, he does not take it well. By now he's forty-six – not too late to start again, I suppose, especially given there'll be a lot of women in similar boats – but he doesn't. Instead, his old interest in spiritualism makes a comeback. There was still some of that around after the Second World War – not as much as there'd been after the first one, but some. But he tires of all that soon enough – been there, done that, and more importantly seen through it all. But what happens instead is, he starts getting obsessed with making a fillum that could capture ghosts."

"Capture?" I was thinking of the shapes in the Le Mans film and how they'd swarmed in it.

"Well, you know – take their picture. He figured that if we could film infra-red and ultraviolet light, that we should be able to approach the supernatural in the same way. A different kind of light, he called it. In theory, he said, it should be possible to create a fillum emulsion that'd make it possible to photograph the dead – no fakery, just science."

"I bet that went over well."

"Aye, you can bet on that. He'd become a crank. More to the point, he'd become erratic – he was drinking a lot, and spending more and more time in this lab he'd set up, pissing around with his magic fillum. Once people stop thinking you're reliable, that's it for you. By the end of '54, no-one would touch him."

"1954?" I said. "You're sure about that?"

"Aye. There was a fuss in January '55 when they caught him trying to get in to film the aftermath of the Sutton Coldfield Rail Crash. Can't remember if it was a defunct press card or a forged one, but anyway. He was lucky not to end up in court, but there were a couple of folk there who knew him and still had a wee bit of sympathy. After that, though, he pretty well drops off the radar completely." Paddy shrugged. "Doesn't seem to have been about anything fillum-related in his last years. Died in '59, '60 or '61. They couldn't tell which."

"Eh?"

"He vanished in May 1959. No-one knew where he'd gone. He'd been pretty much living in the lab he'd rented, and once the rent came overdue the landlord went and seized all his gear. It was 1962 before they finally found what was left of him. Some young lovers in a wood got a hell of a nasty shock when they went to find a spot to canoodle. He'd hanged himself from a tree. Wasn't much left, of course – they found what was left of some ID on him, and the teeth were intact so they could use dental records – and the pathologist couldn't pin down the time of death to anything closer than between one and three years before."

"Poor bastard."

"Aye. So anyway, what's the interest?"

I'd been prepared for the question, and answered with most of the truth. "Found some old film footage and the can had his name on it. I was trying to find out if it's genuine."

"Think it is?"

"I think so. It's from '55, anyway."

"Looks like he got away with forging his press pass one last time," said Paddy. "So was that a help?"

"It was."

"Grand. I've emailed you some scans and notes going over what I've told you. Plus my invoice, of course. Mate's rates as ever."

"Thanks, Paddy."

"Welcome. Now when you going to come up and see us?"

"Could arrange something for the New Year, I guess."

"See that you do. It's been way too long. We'll make up the guest room. Bring the girlfriend. If you've got one yet."

"Not right now."

Paddy rolled her eyes. "Never did get over La Starmer, did you? A cunt-struck man is a sad sight to see."

"Oh, bugger off."

She grinned and blew a kiss. "Later, pal. All the best."

———

I paid Paddy and Tony both through PayPal within ten minutes of the end of the video-call – always a good idea to pay promptly – and went through the material Paddy had attached before putting together an email for Danie. *La Starmer*, as Paddy had called her. I didn't send it straight away though, just saved it as a draft and fired off another, shorter one saying simply *video chat?*

5 mins, she emailed back, so I popped to the bathroom – it was dark by then, but every light in the cottage was still on – made a pot of tea, then sat down to wait. A minute or two later I had an incoming video-call.

Danie looked more frazzled than ever, but with the kind of nervous energy that comes out of a lot of work. "What have we got?" she said.

I gave her a précis of what I'd learned from Paddy. "At an educated guess," I said, "Coldgrain managed to wangle his way into the press enclosure at Le Mans, and the film in his camera had been treated with this special emulsion he'd been working on. And it actually worked."

"But why go there? I don't get it. He wanted to film ghosts, there were plenty of places he could have gone for that – crime scenes, places like that. Why go to all the hassle of trying to get in with the press?"

I'd given that some thought while putting together my draft email. " Coldgrain wouldn't have wanted to catch something on film only to have it dismissed as a fake. So he gets footage of something that a dozen other cameramen shoot at the same time – get it developed straight away and if there *is* a ghost on the film no-one can claim it's been doctored or staged."

"I'm sure someone would," said Danie. "That could be it though. But how could he know there'd be a crash?"

"I doubt he did. There had been fatal accidents at Le Mans, though. Maybe he thought there might be something left over from one of them. Or that he'd catch a new one – which he did."

"Doesn't look as though he got round to telling the world, though, does it?"

"Are you surprised?"

Danie grimaced. "Fuck no."

"So, what have you got?"

"I got copies of Heggie's accounts, that's what. He was pretty meticulous about it all, so they were easy to find."

"Find what?"

"The four purchases he made from shops in the Lake District this year," she said, grinning. "Which, if you remember, was where he said he'd got the film from."

"Ah, right."

"Two of them were from the same place, so we've got three possibilities. I'll email them over to you shortly."

"Me?"

She nodded. "I've got a job here in London. I'm not gonna be able to get away for the next few days – besides, I'm gonna try and sweet-talk my police contacts to see if I can get access to Heggie's effects. He said he bought a job lot of stuff, so maybe there's some more of Coldgrain's things at his place."

"Something that might shed a bit more light, you mean?"

"Yeah. After what happened to Heggie – well, I don't want to be next. Do you?"

It was my turn to say "Fuck no."

"Well, then. And anyway, you're nearer to the Lakes than me. Maybe you can dig up something if you follow the trail. All Coldgrain's stuff must have gone somewhere. I've a hard time believing it just sat in an antique shop in Keswick or wherever for nearly seventy years. Haven't you?"

"When you put it like that, yeah. So maybe there's family, or someone who might know something."

"There you go." Danie gestured, as though to say *See? I'm always right.* "So you have a crack at that, and I'll do my thing here."

"Okay."

I set off for the Lakes the first thing the next morning, and it was a good thing I did. A new storm came blowing in from the Atlantic, surpassing all estimates and lashing the north-west with hurricane-force winds and torrential rain. The train was halted a little north of Lancaster, and was going nowhere till the storm abated.

I battled through flying sheets of water and flurries of debris blown off the streets to the nearest hotel, only to find it fully occupied. Several attempts later and fairly sure I was about to develop pneumonia, I found one with vacancies, and was just in time to book the last remaining room.

Once in there, I turned its heating on and hung up my sodden clothes to dry before running the hottest shower possible. Which wasn't that hot given the state of the hotel plumbing, but I managed to chase the chill from my bones, and after that brewed several cups of hot, sweet tea. That went a long way to restoring a sense of well-being.

I climbed into the narrow single bed, leaving the bedroom light on, and pulled the covers over my head, partly so I could get to sleep and partly because that, too, felt safer – as any child knows, there's nothing like being completely covered by a duvet for shielding you from the claws of monsters and the blows of axe murderers. Even so, rest was fitful and hard to come by at first; the hotel wasn't a quiet place.

For one thing, the pipes knocked and the building constantly seemed to be creaking and settling; for another, the winds were howling outside at near-deafening volume – and sounded unpleasantly like voices, more particularly the kind that might well have been heard in the devastated stands at Le Mans after Levegh's car had exploded. The rain crashed in rattling waves on the hotel roof and against the windows, so loudly and sharply it sounded as though it'd given way to hail.

And, of course, the hotel was full up, with no shortage of comings and goings in the corridor – quiet footsteps and heavy clomping ones and voices too, some loud and some hushed. I was used to the quiet of my cottage, so it was hard to settle for some time. At least until the comforting thought occurred to me that I was among people, and that there might be some security in that. Not long afterwards, I managed to get to sleep.

The storm had passed over by the next morning, but it wasn't until the afternoon that the trains were running again. When I reached Penrith, I booked into another hotel – given the weather reports, there was no way I was heading back home the same day.

Besides, the three antique shops I needed to visit were in different villages, all some way apart. I guessed Heggie had made something of a working holiday of it, combining business and pleasure – potter around the sights and distractions, while nosing around in any antique shop he came across in search of new stock.

The Penrith hotel had wi-fi, and – miracle of miracles – it actually worked. I emailed Danie to let her know what had happened, then set about poring over Google Maps to gauge the relative proximity and ease of access of the three shops and work out an itinerary. She rang me while I was in the middle of that.

"Hi, Danie."

"Ash? Jesus, are you okay?"

"Yeah, yeah. Just the joys of modern rail travel." I frowned. Danie's voice sounded shakier than I'd ever heard it before. Maybe it was the line, which was a little crackly, after all. Faint rustling and whispering sounds. "Are *you?*"

She gave a weak, shaky laugh. "I've been better."

"What is it?"

"Chris," she said. "He's missing."

"Missing?" She didn't answer and I sat there for nearly a minute trying to think of what to say. "What happened?" I said.

"The police got in touch," said Danie. "Bit of a coincidence, apparently, my name popping up again. There was a power failure at his house this morning – set a bunch of alarms off. When the cops got there, there was no answer, so they broke in – place was all locked up and secure. Power came back on, and… so did the film projector."

"Oh Christ."

"The film was finished, anyway, so nobody saw anything. None of the police, I mean."

"But Chris would have?"

"I expect so."

"Was it…"

"What do you think?" Danie's voice was sharp and ragged. "Yes," she said after a moment. "It was the Le Mans footage. Everything was – there was a bottle of brandy, a glass, and…"

"And?"

"A box of tissues and a bottle of lube."

I couldn't help it. I started laughing hysterically at that, which I expect would have got me some funny looks if I hadn't been alone in the bedroom. "We did warn him," I said.

"Yes, we did," said Danie, but I could tell that wasn't easing her conscience any more than it was mine. After a brief silence, she said: "We should have burned that fucking film."

"Yeah," I said. "We should've. But we didn't."

Danie didn't answer, and I couldn't think of much to add. All too often, we never know the moment that's going to change our lives; at other times, of course, we do, but the worst ones are the ones where you look back and realise that you should have. As I said before, it hadn't been a great choice, but it had been a choice all the same: the right thing, costly though it would have been, and the wrong one. We'd chosen wrongly, and my healthily improved bank balance seemed pretty meaningless now. I suspected Danie would have preferred her only problems to be a chronic lack of funds as well. An old Biblical quote came to mind: *for what profits a man if he gains the whole world but loses his own soul?* Another quotation followed on the heels of that, this time from Thomas Hobbes: *Hell is truth seen too late.*

"Right," Danie said at last. She was trying to sound her old, confident self and I remembered that phone call of hers that had started it all: brash, breezy, confident, in control. Hurricane Danie. La Starmer. The D. "We'd better... crack on. See what we can find."

"Right," I said. "Right."

"Check back later?"

"Okay. Danie?"

"Yeah?"

I love you, I said. Or I wanted to. The words were very nearly out of my mouth. But at the last instant, I stopped myself from saying them. I probably should have. It felt like goodbye. It felt like the last time. And maybe that's why I didn't. To say it out loud would have been the final admission that we were fucked. "Keep the lights on," I said. "It seems to help."

I think that even a day or two before, she would have pretended not to know what I meant. But we were past that point now. Long past it. "Okay," she said. "Yeah. Good thinking. You as well, right?"

"Yeah."

Neither of us mentioned brownouts or power cuts. Or what had happened in Heggie's house.

I love you, I wanted to say again. But all I said was "Speak to you later, then."

"Okay. Look after yourself Ash."

"Bye."

"Bye."

The phone went silent in my ear. I slipped it into my pocket, and went back to planning my day.

Public transport in the area was pretty sporadic – the bus services didn't have the frequency of those in the big city, and that was without adding the malign influences of cuts in government funding and disruption from weather conditions. Luckily I was able to track down a care hire firm and rent a Landrover for the day – something capable of off-road travel seemed like a good bet under the circumstances – and set off.

My first stop was out near Bassenthwaite; it was the furthest of the shops from me, but it was also the one Heggie had visited twice. Unfortunately, it quickly proved to sell practically nothing but old postcards and photographs. The plump, kindly old lady who ran the place couldn't recall the last time she'd had any old reels of film in stock, if indeed she ever had. She remembered Heggie, though. He'd been something of a regular, since her speciality had been exactly his. He'd been so taken with her wares on that occasion he'd made two trips. She was sorry to hear he'd passed away – that was all I told her. I spared her the circumstances.

I left her mourning one of her best customers and drove back towards Penrith, stopping on the way in Keswick to visit the second shop. I wasn't sure what Heggie could have seen in the place, which seemed to be more bric-a-brac than anything else, with the only wares that would have interested him being a stack of old magazines in one corner, so I mentioned his name to the thin, greasy-looking man behind the counter. With a grin, he beckoned me towards the rear of the shop and slipped through a bead curtain into a back room. I hesitated before going, and not just because the man's appearance and behaviour didn't inspire trust: there were no windows in the back room, and it was very dark. The shadows in the corners seemed to stir. He looked back at me, frowned, then switched on a light, at which point I followed him, although I put a hand in my pocket and got a grip on my car keys just in case I needed to press them into service as a weapon.

Carefully stored in sealed plastic crates, and individually held in plastic wallets, was as extensive a selection of vintage porn as ever I've seen. Some of the pictures were Victorian, while the most recent stuff consisted of magazines from the 1950s. I did wonder for a moment if there might be a Coldgrain connection, given the rumours Paddy had quoted about his father

– and had Victor spent his final years eking out his earnings with a sideline in cheesecake pictures? I had a hard time imagining images of the things from Le Mans interesting the editors of *Health and Efficiency, Beautiful Britons, Spick* or *Span* magazines.

"This is what Mr Heggie was always after," the thin man said, taking out another crate. "Couldn't get enough, he couldn't. Dunno if it was a regular customer or just his thing. Are you acting for him? Let him know I'm expecting a big haul of this stuff."

I held off telling him about Heggie's death; all I'd told him was that I was a friend of his. The crate was full of Parisian postcards from the 1920s, a cursory flick through of which reminded me that the French had a reputation for a considerably more open attitude to sex than the British.

"Did he ever buy any films from you?" I asked.

"Films?" The thin man sucked his teeth. "Not really, not as such. Not my line, you see. There was just the one time—"

"Yeah?"

"Yeah. Something from Germany. Weimar Republic, you know, 1920s? He always liked that period. The Jazz Age and all that." He sniggered. "Dirty buggers, the Germans…"

"Yeah, I think he mentioned that. The film, I mean."

I bought a couple of the postcards and left. I've still got them, although I keep meaning to throw them away or burn them. Not that I think I'm in any danger from them; it's just that I'd really rather they're not found with my dead body. I do have some standards; not many, but some.

I drove back into Penrith, bought a burger for lunch and checked my phone for messages from Danie. Nothing so far. I picked up a coffee to drink on the way and set off again.

The last shop was on the opposite side of the town, although not as far from it as the first had been, in a tiny hamlet about a mile north-east of Melmerby. It would be a short drive back to the hotel when I was done here; with or without answers, I'd be glad to get some rest.

The shop was on the High Street – pretty much the only street – of a tiny Lakeland village. I almost turned around then and there when I saw the sign above the door: LLOYD'S RARE AND SECONDHAND BOOKS. But I'd come this far, and I'd found no other leads, so in I went.

I saw I'd been right to do so straight away, because Lloyd's didn't just sell books – although books did take up the bulk of the shop space, which stretched further back than I'd expected. But there were also shelves and tables to one side of the space, stacked with any number of items. There were old clocks, the ancient yellowed skull of some animal – a walrus, according to the card that accompanied it, lettered in precise block capitals. It was minus its tusks, otherwise it would have been a fairly easy guess. An old lamp, a samovar… further down there was a glass case inside which were an assortment of fearsome-looking knives and swords on one shelf, a selection of old flintlock and percussion pistols (OBSOLETE CALIBRE, read a script in the same neat capitals as the card that had accompanied the walrus skull, NO LICENCE REQUIRED) on the next, and then another shelf that took up most of the room inside the case, housing the real treasures.

Mounted on dummy heads were a spiked Prussian police-issue *Pickelhaube* and a First World War leather flying helmet, complete with goggles; beside these was a marble statue about two feet high of what I guessed to be some sort of mythical beast or demon, although it resembled nothing I'd ever heard or read about (and I've read more of my share of folklore and mythology, partly for pleasure and partly for work); I only knew that it was both brilliantly executed and bloody horrible to look at (although still quite definitely preferable to some things I'd seen of late.) Not to mention eye-wateringly well-endowed.

Next to the ugly statuette was a string puppet of about the same size, representing a small child – the paintwork was lovely, if a little chipped, but I moved quickly on because I've never liked those things. Beside that was a beautiful Harrach glass jug with gold inlay around the rim and a handle in the shape of a black serpent. Danie would have loved it, and under other circumstances I would have thought of buying it for her. Well, at least until I saw the price tag. Perhaps later, if we could get through what was happening without suffering Chris or Heggie's fates. It would be a way to celebrate, I supposed.

But then I forgot about the Harrach jug, because next to it stood an old-fashioned film projector. And that was when I knew I'd come to the right place.

"Are you looking for anything in particular?"

I jumped and nearly fell, but the white-haired, bespectacled old man who'd spoken held out an arm to steady me. "I do apologise," he said. "People never seem to hear me coming."

He looked as ordinary and harmless as you could wish for, or he would have. But I'd turned around a little more quickly than he'd anticipated, so I caught, very briefly, the cold gleam in his eyes as he registered and, more importantly, relished the small fright he'd given me.

It was a very brief impression, but rightly or wrongly it put me on my guard. Danie had called me naïve more than once, but now and again I'd get a feeling about someone, either good or bad. And I'd learned the hard way not to ignore it.

"That's okay," I said. The old man released my arm. "Sorry, you were saying?"

"I just wondered if you might be looking for anything in particular, sir. I have a great deal of stock not on public display, or that I can source quite quickly." He cocked his head. "In my trade, I like to think that I can tell a browser from a gentleman in search of something… specific."

There was a head-spinning moment when I was sure he knew – knew everything. What had happened, why I was here. Then it was gone, and I was just looking at a pleasant-seeming old man again. I wondered if the days of stress and broken sleep were making me hallucinate; I decided not to go down that road, as given the way things were just now I'd soon be unable to tell fantasy from reality.

"Yeah, actually, I am," I said. "I think a friend of mine bought something from you, earlier in the year?"

"Oh?" The old man raised his bushy eyebrows.

"Yeah. Malcolm Heggie? I don't know if you—"

"Oh, of course, yes, I remember Mr Heggie. A Scottish gentleman, if memory serves?"

"That's right."

"A fondness for old photographs. And occasionally films."

Again, it was as if he knew. "That's right," I said. "It was the film – the films – that I was interested in."

"I see." He nodded, then offered a small, gnarled hand. "Henry Lloyd."

"Ashok Dhillon," I said, although I didn't feel entirely comfortable giving him my name. No way around it, though.

"Good to meet you, Mr Dhillon. I have a selection of films – it isn't huge, but there are some interesting specimens…"

"Well, the film he bought was – it's more about the person who made the film, you see."

"Ah, yes. Now, wait. I should remember this. It was written on the reel I sold him. A fairly uncommon name." He raised a hand and closed his eyes for a moment. "Yes, that was it. Coldgrain. Am I right? V. Coldgrain. Yes, I have some of Mr Coldgrain's things." He gestured towards the case. "That projector, for a start."

"Does it work?"

"Oh, yes, of course. I make a point of ensuring *everything* in my shop is in working order." Mr Lloyd motioned towards the rear of the shop. "Would you like to step into my office? I shall consult the oracle for you."

"The oracle?"

Mr Lloyd chuckled. "My inventory, Mr Dhillon. I'll see exactly what items of Mr Coldgrain's are in my possession. And we can proceed from there."

Mr Lloyd's office was a small, cosy back room with well-worn, comfortable armchairs and a table on which rested a kettle, a jar of instant coffee, a bag of sugar and a freshly-opened pint of milk. No tea was in evidence. I'm not much of a coffee drinker but accepted a cup for politeness' sake while Mr Lloyd pulled up a small folding table and switched on the Mac that rested on it. It was strange seeing such a piece of advanced technology there; it didn't seem to fit in among so much that belonged to the past.

Mr Lloyd glanced up at me and gave a reedy little chuckle. "One must move with the times," he said. "And it does make matters more convenient."

"Except during a power cut."

"Oh, I keep it plugged in, as you see, and it has an excellent battery life. But, you're here about Victor Coldgrain." He polished his glasses and peered through the thick lenses at the screen. "Let's see what I've got. If I recall correctly... ah, yes."

He picked up his coffee cup and took a delicate sip. The silence stretched out uncomfortably.

I cleared my throat. "Did you – find something?"

"Mm?" He blinked. "Oh, yes, of course. How silly of me. Completely forgot. I must be growing senile."

I doubted that, somehow. In fact, I doubted that Mr Lloyd had ever forgotten anything important for any length of time. He just enjoyed spinning things out, playing his little games with people. A small taste of power can be very intoxicating.

"Coldgrain," he murmured, "Coldgrain. Ah, yes, here we are. Provenance. Prove*nance*," he said, giving the last syllable a Francophone emphasis. "I purchased several trunks of material at an auction three years ago. The previous owner had died without any heirs or assigns, and she'd also, it seems, been an inveterate hoarder. The trunks were of particular interest to me because they'd belonged to her father – who was, if memory serves, a landlord in his day. Renting out both residential and business properties."

"Coldgrain's lab," I said.

"Hm?" Mr Lloyd took off the spectacles and polished them again. "You may be right, you may be right. The gentleman was quite meticulous in his way: he'd pack any materials he seized into crates, labelled with the name of the relevant defaulting tenant. He seems to have been a bit of a hoarder too: wasn't much for selling things on, anyway. Of course, he may have passed away before having the chance to do so with these items. There were two trunks of items belonging to Victor Coldgrain. The contents of one, of course, you've already seen – the projector, that is."

"Only the projector?" I said. "Was there anything else?"

"Ah, there was, yes. A reel of film. I'd originally intended to sell it along with the projector, but Mr Heggie was only interested in the film itself. Had his own projector at home, of course."

"Was that all there was?"

"In *that* trunk," smiled Mr Lloyd, "yes." He didn't blink, and I thought of a lizard or a snake.

"What about the other trunk?"

"Ah, the other trunk." Mr Lloyd replaced his glasses. "Well, this was a sort of loose assortment of items. Pieces of laboratory equipment and some books – journals, I think, belonging to Mr Coldgrain." He made to remove the spectacles once more, then made a big show of peering at the screen again. "Oh, yes – and another reel of film."

"Another reel?" I said.

"Mm. So it would appear. I should have spotted that before. Mr Heggie might have been interested. How *is* Mr Heggie, by the way?"

He said it very casually, still peering at the screen, but I had a feeling he already knew the answer. Again, though, I played his game because I had to. "He's dead."

"Really? Goodness. Dearie me. I am sorry to hear it. He was a good customer of mine."

I waited for him to ask something else – what had happened, or even whether it was connected with the matter in hand – but he didn't. He just returned his attention to the screen. "If the trunk is of interest to you," he said, "I can let you have it at a fair price."

The price he named wasn't that fair, but I think he knew that I was in no position to refuse or even haggle. I think Mr Lloyd knew a great deal, and very little of it good. When I accepted, he nodded, then added: "Oh, and if you're a completist, then for an extra fifty pounds I'll include the projector too. It's worth more than that, but as a gesture of good will… and of course, if you don't have a projector of your own but want to view the film very quickly, for whatever reason, then as I say every mechanical device in my shop is sold in full working order."

―――

I paid and I got out of there, as soon as Mr Lloyd had finished helping me load the trunk and projector into my car. He was stronger than he looked, despite his age. He stood in the street and waved to me as I drove off: I saw his rumpled figure receding in the rear view mirror, just a kindly, harmless old man, and hoped I never had cause to see him again.

———

Back at the hotel, one of the porters helped me tote the trunk up to my room. The lab equipment – bottles, retorts and that kind of thing – were still in the boot of the Landrover; I'd stopped on the way back to Penrith and removed them from the trunk, making enough space to manhandle the projector in.

The lights kept flickering on and off; the porter told me there'd been a brown-out earlier. The power supply was supposed to be okay for now, but there'd still been a few little 'flickers and fluctuations', as he put it, since.

As long as the lights didn't go out completely, I didn't mind. A bigger source of concern was that both the broadband connection and all mobile phone service in the vicinity were down. Admittedly, they could be fitful anyway out in this neck of the woods – I'd been lucky before – but I badly wanted to hear Danie's voice just then.

I hung a DO NOT DISTURB sign on the door and unlocked the crate. For the time being, I ignored the projector, and did my best to ignore the remaining reel of film. I glanced once at its case, at the yellowed slip of paper taped to it, just to confirm that the writing on it was the same, faded, spidery writing as on the Le Mans footage. It was. There was the name, *Victor Coldgrain*, and underneath that a date – *27/03/1958* – and a single word: *Redbrook*.

I'd no idea what that meant, or if I really wanted to know. That question was irrelevant anyway: I didn't have a choice. But for the time being I could ignore the reel. Maybe I wouldn't have to watch it. There were the journals to consider.

I made a strong, sweet cup of tea, sat up on the bed with my back against the wall, and started reading the journals.

The first journal began in 1947 and didn't offer much in the way of a reward. It was mostly filled with chemical formulae and scribblings about what as far as I could tell was some fairly abstruse philosophy, with forays into occultism. Not that Coldgrain seemed to be religious, in that or any other sense: his approach was scientific, or striving to be. I got the sense that he was plundering occult and alchemical works for anything that might give him a direction to go in, and with very little initial success.

It was very clearly a record of his work and nothing more. 'Berkeley Square, No. 50: 100 feet of film exposed and fifty photographs taken over a 48 hour period. No result whatever. Glamis Castle: 100 feet of film exposed and fifty photographs taken over a 48 hour period. Nothing. Tower of London: 100 feet of film exposed and fifty photographs taken over a 48 hour period. <u>ABSOLUTELY BLOODY FUCK-ALL</u>.' The nib of his pen had splintered at that point, leaving a speckle of ink on the page.

It was the only moment in the first journal where Coldgrain displayed even a hint of the frustration and grief that must have been driving him. Immediately afterward, the level, objective tone reasserted itself as he began new experiments, an altered or completely different formula. He was both obsessive and methodical: the one thing he didn't question was that he'd find an answer.

The first journal ended in mid-1951, having provided no new information. The second, covering the next three years of Coldgrain's life, was a little more revealing. As his experiments continued – and continued also to bear no fruit – the scientific record was interrupted more and more often by outbursts of a more personal nature as his sorrow and frustration spilled out onto the page.

———

4ᵗʰ November 1953

Last week was bad: two failures within ten days of one another. I was so sure I only needed to modify that particular formula to get a result, but no. I must begin again, from scratch.

I'm close to giving up. I don't just mean the experiments, either. I mean everything. Spent several days pondering not on which combination of chemicals might be most efficacious, but which method of suicide. A rope, perhaps, or opening my veins in a hot bath? A dose of drugs such as morphia? Poison I will not consider – strychnine, arsenic, all of those can be horribly painful, and I don't want that. I am, I've got to admit, rather cowardly in these matters. It's dying, not death, that I'm afraid of – especially if, as is seeming more and more probable, death is nothing but oblivion, the end, the extinction of the personality, and all the hopes and stories of afterlives, heavens and hells nothing more than illusions, dreams and fairytales. If it is just the end, it's nothing to be afraid of. Everyone I love is gone, so why should I persist?

On the heels of that it did occur to me, however – out of the depths of my despair – that perhaps my error hasn't been in the composition of my emulsion, but in trying to compose it at all. Perhaps whatever future state awaits us – if any does – is fundamentally unknowable in this life. Perhaps by its nature no way exists to record it by means of the material sciences and provide the kind of hard, inarguable, easily replicable proof that would convince both myself and others. Perhaps instead my energies should have been directed towards building a new life for myself – looking towards the future, rather than the past.

Perhaps, indeed, but that is easily said. Achieving it is something else. I'm no longer young – in fact, I feel old beyond my years. Sybil and Julian – if one of them had died, but not the other, it might have been different. Which one would I have chosen, if I could, to survive? Oh, Julian, of course. It would have had to have been – Sybil would never have wanted otherwise. But Julian as he was, of course, before Dieppe. God, he was better dead than as that awful, ravaged thing they brought back to us. It would have been a mercy to have let him die.

No, I can't look to the future – not yet, anyway. I'm not a theologian, but I am familiar with the religious concept of despair – that is, to believe oneself to be beyond salvation. The desperate were considered to be potential suicides, and despair was considered to be an unforgivable sin. Salvation and damnation are just words to me – although that may change if I ever succeed – but I do despair of ever being able to be a husband again, let alone a parent. I'm not too old for that, if I wanted to – but I couldn't bear it, not after knowing the pain of losing a child. Not unless I knew that there was something more than this life.

And so, I return to my experiments. From a scientific point of view, I know that blind faith is a failing: I can only conclude what the evidence shows. But at the same time, I have to believe that there's a solution and that I'll find it. It's the only thing that can still sustain me.

Shortly after, there were notes on a new formula, new plans, new experiments, and Victor Coldgrain was back on the horse again. But the process was cyclic: here was a new hope and up his spirits went, only to plunge back down in failure. There were long stretches of nothing but results, recorded drily, and then there'd be another outburst of frustration. And so it dragged on, to the conclusion of the second journal in December 1954.

And then I reached the final journal. I knew, somehow, that this would yield something. There'd been a rising sense of tension in the second book, like the feeling in the air before a thunderstorm finally breaks.

And, of course, this journal had to cover the period leading up to Le Mans.

From the first page, things were different.

I've decided. This is it, this year. Make or break. I no longer have the resources – not only financial but psychological or spiritual – to sustain my quest beyond that. And so it's very simple. I'll either achieve positive, undeniable results – prove beyond doubt that there's existence beyond death – or else I'll put an end to things. December the 31st, 1955, will mark my farewell to this world, and I shan't miss it. Unless, unless, unless. Unless I capture something on film. A ghost, a spirit, some token of the beyond. If I succeed, I shall continue to live. What I'll actually do then I don't know. That will depend on the results, I think. But that's a question that will wait until later. It will be enough, to paraphrase George Bernard Shaw, that there is a beyond. My problem now, at least, is a far simpler one.

Victor Joseph Coldgrain
1st January 1955 A.D.

He'd signed it, I thought, as though it were an official statement – that, or a legally binding contract. I suppose that in its way it was both of those.

And so the cycle I was familiar with from the earlier journals began again. New formulae, preparation of the emulsion, treatment of the film, use of the film – and then failure. And then, beginning again.

26ᵗʰ March 1955

I may have misconceived another part of my approach. I've spent a great deal of time filming the traditional 'haunted houses'. Quite apart from anything else, these locations are so obvious that some would accuse me of fakery purely on those grounds – Coldgrain the sensationalist, making his cheap cinematic penny dreadfuls. Imagine if I actually succeeded, only to be disbelieved. Oh, of course, I'd still know, and that might give me some sort of peace. The sure and certain knowledge Julian and Sybil aren't forever lost to me. But that won't be enough, not any more. I've been mocked and pitied and dismissed enough. And there are others like me. And for God's sake – if there is a God, which life has given me plenty of cause to doubt – as scientific discoveries go, this would be one for the ages, would it not? It would revolutionise our understanding of the world as profoundly as anything Einstein or Crick and Watson have discovered. I need proof that will convince.

And what do we know, truly, of the lives of the dead? All we have, for the most part, is the cant of religion and the fireside tales of folklore – all very well to raise a pleasing frisson on a cold night, in the latter case, but hardly scientific proof. Might the dead not lead existences as complex as our own in life? Might they not wander freely among the living? In which case my camera needs to study more common, everyday settings. But still the same problem arises: how to avoid accusations of fakery?

And the solution has come to me. It was blindingly obvious, in fact: a basic principle of scientific study is that there must be a control, a replica of the experiment conducted minus one essential element in order to observe the contrast. I've neglected that. And I know I'm thought of as little more than a drunken crank these days. But if I can make use of my connection to the newsreels, all might not be lost. My control will be my former colleagues: they'll have footage of the same events.

Later entries bitterly lamented the impossibility of finding employment with any of the newsreel companies, and then over the ignominy and humiliation of being ejected from an event when his press pass proved invalid.

7ᵗʰ May 1955

At least they accepted it as an honest error on my part. Pity, pity – it's a very base coinage, but it bought me out of trouble this time. I suspect it's a very limited reserve, though. No matter, no matter. I was able to expose a couple of hundred feet of film before I was found out.

The results are inconclusive. The images on the film may be nothing but shadows. God knows I must guard against wishful thinking at this stage of the game – I want, I need, success in some form. But my proofs must convince others as well as myself. I've got to keep that in mind. How ridiculous and pitiful a figure would I cut if I proudly screened a reel showing only ordinary flickers and scratches and declared them proof of life everlasting? I couldn't bear that. I'm carrying on only by an effort of will as it is.

Nonetheless – nonetheless, I don't think the images are only shadows. I think that I may just have caught something, however imperfectly. So the next step is to isolate the factor that made this emulsion partially work, and then accentuate it. And then, find an occasion on which to use it.

It never seemed to occur to Coldgrain that he could have just shot a reel of film anywhere to see if it got results, and then tried to arrange a proper demonstration later. But he'd been on this trail a long time, and besides, there was no knowing when one of the dead might or might not oblige him with an appearance.

In any case, he spent the weeks following his ejection refining the emulsion formula and treating new reels of film, preparing for his next attempt. He wanted the right occasion, and it didn't take him long to find it.

1ˢᵗ June 1955
All's ready. The emulsion's been perfected, the film's been prepared, and now I have the time and the place. It's

outside Britain, so the embarrassment of being caught a second time with a dud pass might be a little less likely to reach the ears of certain former colleagues. I'm sure I'll be able to pass it off as another case of poor old drunken Coldgrain – not that I want to ruin whatever little reputation I have left. But this pass is a much better forgery; it cost me a great deal of money I can ill afford to spare.

There's always the element of pot luck, of course, in that the film can't capture anything that isn't there to be captured. I'm not referring to the possibility that there are no ghosts, no afterlife, that the phenomenon I'm trying to record simply doesn't exist – although, of course, I can't wholly dismiss that fear. If I could, I wouldn't be where I am: I'd accept without question that there'll be a reunion with Sybil and Julian and carry on with the life I have left. That, or accept they're gone for good – I'm not sure what accommodation, if any, I could come to with existence in that event. But that is where the thought of suicide can be such a balm to an anguished soul.

No, that isn't what I mean. Pot luck doesn't come into that equation: either we continue beyond the body's death, or we do not. Whatever the correct answer, it's an iron and inflexible law, and neither luck, nor prayers, nor tears will alter it.

It's simply a question of whether there'll be any spirits present at that time and place. If it's devoid of them, it'll all be for nothing. But I don't think that will be an issue. If tradition is any guide, those who've met a sudden or violent end are often said to haunt the site of their demise. And Le Mans has claimed its share of lives over the years.

There were three more brief entries before the race itself, but they said nothing that wasn't wholly prosaic: one covered the travel arrangements, and another the question of how to cover as wide an area as possible without arousing suspicion.

The third was dated 11ᵗʰ June, the day of the race itself, and simply said: 'Everything's prepared. I've done all I can. It's all in the lap of the gods now. *In manus tuas, Domine*, as it were. Ha!'

There wasn't another entry until nearly a week later. He'd made three attempts to begin, crossing the first two out after barely half a dozen words, the third after a couple of lines. But at last, he'd managed.

17ᵗʰ June, 1955
Dear God. If ever a man experienced mixed feelings, it's me. So many mixed feelings.

I have… something. A result of a kind. I think it's fair to say, at last, that I have found proof of… what can I say I've found proof of? A life to come? I hope not —I mean, not if what's on the film is supposed to be an example of what we become after death. It's proof, I suppose, that there's more to this existence than the body, at any rate. Than the purely physical. But I must try to remain scientific about it all. The existence of the things I've filmed only proves that beings of an incorporeal nature exist. That doesn't automatically mean that includes any part of us. But I have some sort of evidence, anyway.

But at what price? I thought I was hardened to suffering, that I could just watch and record no matter what I saw. What's that line of Isherwood's? I am a camera with its shutter open, quite passive, recording, not thinking? I honestly thought I was, that I didn't have the capacity to be moved or appalled or frightened any more, except by the results of the work I was doing. I was wrong, though. Oh, at the time, I was in the moment and in the grip of my great obsession, all I could think about was getting to the site of the crash and film – maybe even capture the moment a soul left the body. Of course, all anyone would have seen was some hungry-eyed ghoul filming the carnage. And I suppose I was. I eventually stopped filming and did what I could to help, moving the dead aside and covering them so they had some dignity, aiding or comforting the wounded to the best of my poor ability. I avoided people's eyes. I was afraid they'd seen me earlier and were judging me for it.

But at last I got away, with my reel of precious film. I hid it, kept it safe: I knew I'd have to wait until I got to my lab to develop it, much less view the footage. I was convinced some policeman or official would try to confiscate the film on these grounds or those, but none did. On the ferry, I kept it on me at all times, in a waterproof container, because by then I was terrified that the ferry would sink, and I was determined not to let the sea cheat me of my prize. When I landed at Portsmouth there was once more the terror of confiscation, but at last, at last, I reached my laboratory and immediately set to work developing the negative.

Now, of course, there was a new terror – that the film would be damaged and show no images of any kind, or that the new emulsion wouldn't have worked after all. I was wrong on both counts. I'll describe what I saw as clearly and objectively as I can...

And he does, but I'll spare you it. You already know what he saw.

Coldgrain did his best to interpret what he'd observed. From his description, the things on the film appeared quite solid, but with a translucent quality that made their strange nature clear. He had the same impression of their activities as Danie and I: the long, tattery tendrils the creatures' bodies devolved into had been fastening on the dead and dying. Coldgrain believed that the creatures were feeding on them in some way.

'The herded wolves, bold only to pursue', he quoted; 'The obscene ravens, clamorous o'er the dead; The vultures to the conqueror's banner true, Who feed where Desolation first has fed, And whose wings rain contagion...'

Coldgrain spends a couple of pages trying to work out a rationale – or a cosmology – for the creatures. That, and what to call them. It helps when you can give something a name, I suppose. He describes them as parasites or scavengers, the spiritual equivalent of jackals or vultures. 'But what is it exactly that they feed on? What if we do have eternal souls, but there are creatures that prey on them, devour them, just as predators here on earth do our bodies? What if bad luck or accident means that someone, no matter how good or virtuous a life they led, can simply be... *consumed* by them, if sheer ill chance means that someone like Julian, or Sybil, can be denied a life to come – and I a reunion with them – just because they were in the wrong place at the wrong time?

'Or worse – what if our only role, after death, is to be their prey?'

Based on the jackal/vulture metaphor, he toyed with the name *schakalgeist* – 'jackal-ghost' – maybe looking for a parallel to the term 'poltergeist'. In the end, though, the word he settled on was similar in sound but different in meaning: *schakalgeier* – literally, 'jackal-vulture'. It worked for him, anyway.

After a page or two of these musings, the scientist and technician in Coldgrain reasserts itself. Over the next few days, he screens the film again repeatedly, this time taking careful notes on the behaviour of the *schakalgeier*.

19ᵗʰ June 1955

They feed on both the dying and the dead. I wonder if the dying saw anything? It's possible, perhaps. If I could only interview some of the survivors – some of those who'd come close to dying, perhaps. But what would be the logistics of such an approach? No matter. I'll make a note of it for future reference.

Spiritual scavengers? Or perhaps it's that as the soul is leaving the body, it's vulnerable to them. Like predators keeping watch over an animal's burrow, waiting for it to venture out?

Or perhaps it's the pain and the suffering, the anguish, that they feed on. No, this is no good. All speculation. I'll screen the film again tomorrow and see what conclusions I can draw – it's too late tonight, and I'm too tired, and my old brain's buzzing with ideas and possibilities. Tomorrow. With fresh eyes.

20ᵗʰ June 1955

I'm starting to feel as much of a ghoul as the schakalgeier themselves, poring over the carnage on the film. I'm no clearer on what it is they're feeding on; I can only speculate. I'd need to learn far more about their nature.

And while this breakthrough – and it is a breakthrough – is fascinating, I must remember that I started this for a very specific reason. This is a sideshow at best. But nonetheless an intriguing one. Whenever I look at the film, more appears to be there.

One possibility that appalls me but refuses to be dismissed: what if the schakalgeier, are, in fact, us? If there is an afterlife, and they're what we become? Speculation. Unprovable. But dear God don't let it be true.

Another screening tomorrow. Perhaps more than one. Wring every drop of information from the footage, and then I must focus on moving on, decide the next stage of my research. I could show what I have, see what results I get from it. I might be able to convince a few people, perhaps obtain funding for further research – but I expect the film will be dismissed as fake. I must act quickly in any case; it's been almost a fortnight since the disaster and the longer the interval, the more easily trickery can be claimed.

Until tomorrow.

There was no entry for the 21st, though, or the 22nd. When the journal resumed on the 23rd, Coldgrain's handwriting looked shakier than ever before.

23rd June 1955
I've said that whenever I studied the Le Mans footage, I observed images or events that I previously hadn't. I

assumed at first I was simply noticing details I'd missed in the initial shock of seeing the schakalgeier, but I think I knew the truth long before I admitted it to myself. I denied it only because it sounds insane.

Observation seems to be the key. Some people derive pleasure and fulfilment from tormenting others. I think the schakalgeier derive much more. I think it's how they feed, although I don't pretend to understand how. But you can't torment someone who doesn't know you exist: they batten on the freshly-dead and dying because they can be perceived by them. Wherever there's death and suffering, they have a chance to feed.

On the film, the schakalgeier attach themselves to their victims and grow increasingly substantial for a brief period, then fade away again, presumably when their victims pass beyond their reach, be it into some future state or oblivion.

That's the pattern of behaviour I captured at Le Mans. However, they have begun to break out of these patterns — only for a few seconds at a time, but with each screening, they do so for longer. The footage didn't appear different at each screening. It was different, because the images of the schakalgeier are not a static recording of a past event. I didn't capture them on the film; I connected them to it, and, through it, to me.

Not only can they move of their own volition within the footage, but they're also aware of me. I had to stop the film during the last viewing, because it looked — and I'm fully aware of how insane this sounds — as though they were about to break out of the picture on the screen and emerge into the lab.

Despite stopping the film, I think their activities have already begun to spread beyond it. Last night, I heard movement in the house. When I went to investigate, I *saw something. It might only have been my imagination. But I have also felt, several times now, the sensation of another presence. Sometimes more than one.*

So it would appear that further research into the afterlife will be indefinitely delayed, in favour of research into repelling, or better still destroying, these creatures. I made a discovery, but not the one I was after. Science can be an ironic business in that respect.

———

Light was key: the *schakalgeier* needed the dark to manifest themselves outside the film. 'Soft light and shadows', he'd written. 'They make use of vagueness and ambiguity to establish a form; by using it to terrorise their prey they gain further strength to maintain that form. Direct light disrupts this process, but they're not helpless against it. Through concerted effort they can extinguish or overload light sources.

'So additional methods are required, but it's a matter of trial and error, which the current situation doesn't really lend itself to. One mistake would be fatal, or worse.

'Religious and occult paraphernalia, as far as I can tell, are worse than useless. Other than light, the salt circle's the only effective defence I've found so far. I have no idea as to why.'

The remaining, sporadic entries, spread out over weeks or months, detailed unsuccessful attempts to permanently rid Coldgrain of the *schakalgeier*. 'I admit I'm close to despair,' said one. 'I've almost given up several times, because all I seem able to do is ward them off for a time. They're not going to go away of their own accord, not now they've found living prey.

And sooner or later there'll be a power cut, or I'll accidentally break the salt circle, or they'll find a way through.

'If they could only kill me, it wouldn't be so bad. But if they were able to get to me, I'm afraid they could carry me away with them. Take me to wherever they normally exist. I don't know how long I'd survive there. Days, months, years. Maybe even forever – I doubt time and ageing work the same. I mustn't believe this. I mustn't. But I'm terribly afraid of it.'

The trial-and-error reports continued, separated by longer and longer gaps. 1955 became '56, then '57, then '58. And then, early in 1959:

'I'm fighting a constant rearguard action; there has to be a way to hit back. To actually *hurt* the bastards in some way.

'I've spent the months trawling through reams of obscure folktales and ghost stories, in the hope of finding something that might describe the *schakalgeier*. I found too much and too little – cast your net wide enough and you'll find plenty of descriptions that seem to fit, but the mass of information's too vague and contradictory to be of use. But I *did* finally find something, I think.

'On the outskirts of a village in Dorset, not far from Worbarrow Bay, there's a small wooded combe, which according to local tradition was once home to a murderous clan of robbers. They dragged unwary travellers into the woods to rob, rape, kill and devour – a sort of South-of-England version of Sawney Bean. Well, the robbers ultimately came to the usual bad end, but the valley – unsurprisingly, given the legend – has a pretty grim reputation. So the locals have, mostly, left it alone.

'I say "mostly", but there *is* one old building there – 15th or maybe even 14th century. Haven't been able to unearth anything much about its origins. But as far as recent history goes, it was occupied by several occultist and theosophical groups from the late nineteenth century up until just before the last war. It's called Redbrook, which is also the name of the valley and possibly the family, too.

'Anyway, what caught my attention was another legend attached to the valley – that the woods are still supposed to be haunted either by the evil spirits of the robber clan, or the devils they worshipped, who'll carry you off to some terrible place for a fate worse than death. But what struck me here is that I found several stories about the robber ghosts, and the descriptions of them are a) very consistent and b) identical to the *schakalgeier*.

'I've done my best to trace members of the groups that occupied the house. Most of them are long dead – not encouraging! – but one of the two most recent organisations to own the house still exists, and I have the names of several members of the other. I've written to everyone I can trace. They couldn't have been unaware of the valley's reputation, so their objective was presumably either to control or get rid of the *schakalgeier*. Hopefully at least one of them succeeded. But I've still heard nothing and I don't think I can continue to wait. I'm going to have to go there myself and investigate.

'Should I take the camera? If I catch something on film, could that help or will it may make matters worse? Hard to see how it *could*. The *schakalgeier* already have my scent, after all, and barring a miracle – well, not a *miracle*, a *discovery* of some sort, a breakthrough – it's only a matter of time before they have the rest of me too.'

Two further entries detailed Coldgrain's preparations for the trip, and another described a letter he'd received from an occultist group called the Fraternity of Horus. It admitted the Fraternity had purchased Redbrook House in September 1923 as a retreat for their 'adepts', but insisted they'd barely used it, hence their selling the property early the following February. Clearly a lie, as Coldgrain knew several Fraternity members had stayed there, but two of these had committed suicide and the rest were untraceable.

Another group, the Institute for Psychic, Theosophical and Metaphysical Enquiry, had owned the house in the late 1930s and dissolved itself in early 1940. What few reports Coldgrain could find referred to the investigators only by their surnames – Smith, Brown, Wilson – which were mostly too commonplace to provide a useful lead.

The one exception was that of Lucinda Coleflax, the General Secretary of the Society; while she might still be alive, tracing her would be another matter. Coldgrain had written to Coleflax's last known address with scant hope of a reply, and had received none by the March of 1959.

'Every night's a gamble," he wrote. 'When I close my eyes, will I wake up again? And if I do, where will I find myself? I can't put it off any longer. Tomorrow morning, I'm setting off for Dorset.'

The next few pages were blank, but there was one final entry in the book. It was undated and at an angle

across the page, and written in a thin, spidery scrawl.
It read:

I paced the hotel room, then sat back down on the
bed and tried to think. Victor Coldgrain had vanished
two months after visiting Redbrook, but could have
died almost any time between then and 1962. Paddy
had said he'd been identified from personal effects;
there was always the chance they'd included another
diary. I could wait until morning, till I could contact
Danie again, and compare notes.

But the more I considered it, the more forlorn a
hope it sounded. Coldgrain had been little more than
bones: what chance of survival would ink and paper
have had? Besides, his suicide was hardly a hopeful
sign, from our point of view. Then again, his suicide
might have been unrelated to the *schakalgeier*. He'd
been ageing and alone, after all, and still grieving.
People have killed themselves for far less.

Whatever was on the film, he'd said himself that
with the *schakalgeier* already on his trail things could
hardly get worse. But then there was that last journal
entry. On the other hand, he'd gone to Redbrook itself,
right into the lions' den. Surely the film wouldn't be
as dangerous?

That's roughly how I was thinking, anyway – and no, in retrospect, it doesn't sound very convincing to me either. We make our choices without even knowing it sometimes, then grope around for justifications.

I back-and-forthed a little while longer, then set up the projector and, with much cursing and trial and error, fitted the reel. There was no screen, but the wall was blank and off-white enough to serve.

I plugged the projector in, hesitated one last time, although I was more worried about Lloyd's claim that everything in his shop was in full working order. He wasn't exactly the most trustworthy of men and I didn't consider death by electrocution as an acceptable means of escaping the *schakalgeier*. But I threw the switch, and a square of light appeared on the wall. A flurry of numbers flickered across it, and the film began to play.

It begins halfway down a steep, wooded slope. The camera sweeps from left to right, then back again, through one hundred and eighty degrees. Daylight is shining through the trees. It's bright, but there are still shadows in between trees and beside them. They move, but always just too fast to see properly; there's a constant impression of someone ducking back into hiding, not in time to evade detection.

I kept my hand on the off-switch and told myself a shadow is sometimes only a shadow. I set the projector up beside a light switch, so I could banish the darkness at will. Most of it, anyway. Some. Enough. Enough to keep any unwelcome presences at bay. Any *schakalgeier* out there in the dark.

Just a record, I reminded myself. It was just a record to begin with. It was only with repeated viewings, with sufficient observation, that the *schakalgeier* began to move independently and pose a threat to the observer.

How many times did that take? How many times had Coldgrain had to watch the Le Mans footage before they tried to break out of the screen? How many times had he watched this? How strong would they still be after all this time?

Back and forth and back and forth the camera swung; shadows moved and watched between the trees. I saw glints of pallid light, that might or might not have been eyes.

The bottom of the slope. Woods stretch away across the level ground. *The lone and level sands stretch far away.* That was Shelley. *Ozymandias.* The line about *the obscene ravens*, the *vultures who feed where Desolation first hath fed*, was Shelley, too: *Adonais.* I remembered now. I'd had a girlfriend back at Hull, not long after Danie and I broke up following our one attempt at living together. Her name had been Annemarie. An English Lit student. As people often are at that age, she'd been crazy about the Romantics – Byron, Keats, and old Percy Bysshe. *Adonais* had been written after Keats' death: Annemarie had told me that verse had been directed at critics who'd attacked Keats while he lived, praising him only now he was dead.

Nice girl, Annemarie. Kind. She'd been genuinely in love with me. If I'd been able to forget Danie, we might even have married. Kids, a home; we might still be together, even now. But she hadn't been Danie, and soon Danie and I were back together again, or as together as we'd ever be. Friends with benefits. Annemarie had cried. Said I'd broken her heart. And

I had. I was a bastard. I shouldn't have. Hell is truth seen too late.

But I was where I was, and it was too late for regret. For better or worse, I couldn't get Danie out of my blood; even now, I might still have sacrificed myself to save her. Assuming either of us were eligible for salvation of any kind.

The empty woods; the shifting shadows. The camera turned this way, then that. Saw nothing conclusive. Nothing you could be certain about. Now it pointed back up the slope Coldgrain had just descended. Light flashed through the trees and I glimpsed three tall shapes, like hooded monks, looking down from above. Only for a moment, before they were gone.

The camera kept rolling for several seconds, not moving – maybe Coldgrain glimpsed them too – then swung away and followed a narrow, twisting desire-line through the trees. The picture bounced, the camera dipping at intervals towards the uneven, root-buckled path. At last, it came up and steadied on something through the trees.

The house was about three quarters of the way down the slope, a grey, functional-looking two-storey structure with a gabled roof. It must have stood in a clearing originally, but now trees sprouted only a couple of yards from its outer walls.

Coldgrain followed the remains of a path up the slope; the picture wobbled but remained steady. At the front, a double doorway gaped open: a hungry, toothless mouth. The windows were the sockets of torn-out eyes. The camera zoomed in on the roof; most of its slates were gone, leaving only bare, rotten timbers. Redbrook House looked close to complete collapse.

The shot widened out again, then swept across the front of the building, zooming in on the doorway and each of the windows in turn. Blackness filled the screen whenever it did; I was so sure something would lunge out of it that I nearly switched off the projector twice. But then the camera pulled out again, and Coldgrain began circling the house.

He picked his way through weeds and brambles. Chunks of render had fallen off the walls to expose crumbling stone. At the back of the house he once again zoomed the camera in and out of the windows, and then the hole where the back door had been. Something pale moved in the darkness – but it was the beam of a torch. Coldgrain was shining it into the house. The camera moved closer, and I thought he was about to go in, but then he switched off the torch and moved on around the building.

When he'd circled back round to the front door, he shone the torch inside. The picture rose slightly, then sank down a little, and I realised that Coldgrain had taken a deep breath. The camera pulled out wide again, then moved forward. The darkness swallowed us.

The camera dipped and wobbled about, then came up again. Now a circle of dull light shone directly ahead of it; I guessed Coldgrain had clipped the torch to a fixture on the machine.

The house was little more than a shell. The wood-panelled walls and wooden ceilings had almost completely rotted away. The floor was also littered with gaping holes, plus heaps of debris that had fallen through from above; Coldgrain's progress into the building was slow and fitful. The staircase, too, had collapsed. Coldgrain stood at the bottom, tracking up and down the remaining steps. Even if there had been anything left upstairs, there was no way of getting up there.

Light gleamed down the hallway from up ahead, through the hole of the back doorway. Coldgrain picked his way through the wreckage towards it, into the kitchen. At least he was on more solid ground here: the floor was stone-flagged. The walls were stone, too. An abandoned Aga rusted in one corner, and there was a Belfast sink, shrouded in cobwebs.

In one corner, there was another doorway. Coldgrain moved towards it, probing it with the torch. The light found walls, and stone steps – damp and glistening, but solid. The camera angled downwards: the steps wound away, out of sight.

There was a long pause, the camera frame wobbling slightly as Coldgrain hesitated at the top of the steps. Then he moved forward and started down – slowly, because the steps were slimy with moss. When he reached the bottom the camera dipped and swung about, capturing sections of floor, walls and ceiling, as if Coldgrain was afraid to look at the cellar directly or focus on any single feature for long. But finally it steadied and came up, and he began, slowly and methodically, to record its surroundings.

Redbrook House had been built on top of a natural cavern. Maybe those long-ago robbers had used it as a den. Or a larder. The walls were living rock; I could see markings on them, but I couldn't make them out in any detail.

Like the steps, the stone-flagged floor was damp and mossy. In the centre of the floor, a wide circle had been chiselled in the stone. Candle-holders surrounded it, caked in rust. Coldgrain moved towards the centre of the room and filmed the circle in closer detail. Markings of some kind surrounded it, too, but the occult is one area where my research skills have never really been called on. I had no idea what purpose they were meant to serve.

Next he moved on to the walls. The markings there were cruder, and older-looking. The circle on the floor might have been left by the Fraternity of Horus or the IPTME, but not these. The robbers might have left them, or their victims, or some later band of *schakalgeier*-worshippers of the kind the place must have drawn over the years, in search of who knew what knowledge or power, and they might have been a testament, a prayer or a malediction. It was impossible to make out the words, or even what language they might have been in.

The camera moved suddenly with a jerk, and the picture, even when the shot widened to take in the whole cavern, wobbled. I was sure something had startled Coldgrain, but the cavern remained empty. For a while it remained still, apart from occasional tremors; maybe he was waiting to see if anything showed itself. When nothing did, the camera moved back towards the stairs, at speed. But at the foot of the steps, it swung back round to cover the cellar, and when it did, Coldgrain was no longer alone.

Something lay on the floor in the middle of the circle. It was a person, or it had been. From what I could see, it shouldn't have been alive, but it was still moving. Three tall figures in grey robes stood around it, holding long poles with which they jabbed at the crumpled shape, making it jerk and writhe. They were too tall to be human, and the long arms, and the long, thin hands that grasped the poles, reached almost to the floor.

I still don't really know what I saw at that moment. Perhaps it was some sort of echo from the past, or maybe Coldgrain had accidentally achieved his old ambition of capturing a ghost on film. But it wasn't only the camera that saw: he clearly saw it too. The camera juddered in his hands, then zoomed briefly towards one of the things before pulling back out. When it did, the *schakalgeier* turned, their huge, pale eyes staring directly at the camera.

The picture became a weaving flurry of glimpses, blurs and half-impressions as he blundered up the steps and out through the kitchen towards the back entrance. The next thing I could make out with any clarity, Coldgrain was running through the woods. Trees hurtled up on either side, and the *schakalgeier* now stood openly among them. They watched, hungrily, and from time to time a long arm reached out, but Coldgrain managed to duck or weave to avoid them.

The screen once more became a blur of jumbled images and flickering, almost stroboscopic light as Coldgrain ran between the trees. Now and again a grasping hand or a featureless, pale-eyed face seemed to leap out, but at last a dazzle of clear light burst across the screen and the camera's bouncing and weaving slowed. It wobbled up and down slightly, in time with Coldgrain's ragged breathing. He been close to sixty by then, after all; *schakalgeier* or no, he was lucky to have made it out.

The camera rose and studied an open, sunlit hillside, then widened to take in the gently rolling hills beyond. Even in black and white, it was a lovely scene, especially after what had gone before. But, inevitably, the camera panned around, back the way Coldgrain had come.

The woods below were so dense and dark as to be almost featureless. Not quite, though; I could make out individual trees at the edge, and the shapes that stood between them. The *schakalgeier* moved forward, out of the trees into the sunlight, and then the film jammed in the projector's gate.

The film froze, but they didn't. They swarmed out of the woods, and then one turned and began to swim out of the frozen image towards the surface of the screen, expanding as it did.

The jammed film, strangely, didn't burn. There was no smell. Instead there was a sound, a kind of oddly familiar soft purring noise. I finally recognised it as the sound of slowly ripping fabric, just as I also registered that the swimming *schakalgeier's* head and shoulders were no longer in only two dimensions, but were pushing their way out of the wall. Its shoulders jerked and heaved, as though its arms were pinned at its sides and it was trying to get one free. Its pale blinking eyes stared at me, and I felt the cold blast that came from them.

I had to switch off the projector, but the paralysis I'd suffered at my encounter with them gripped me. The creature in the wall, its body twisted sideways, had managed to pull almost the whole length of its right arm free.

When its hand pulled clear of the wall, the *schakalgeier* lunged, but the paralysis broke and I finally managed to throw the switch. The light cut out, and so did what remained of the projected image, but the *schakalgeier* itself didn't. The upper third of its body was still very visible. Its hand was splayed out as if pressed against an invisible barrier, but it was slowly pushing outward, forward, towards me. I lunged across to the light switch and pressed that too. The light flickered briefly and I was afraid the bulb was about to blow, but it didn't.

I shrank back until I was up against the wall, but the *schakalgeier* continued trying to pull itself free of the wall and its hand continued to push slowly outwards in my direction. A few more seconds and it might have reached me, but by now the thing was beginning to fade in the glare of the electric light. It disappeared slowly, a diminishing stain on the air, still trying to the last to pull itself out of the wall as the substance faded steadily out of it, till it was a vague outline with two whitish smears for eyes, and then not even that. For a minute or so there was a sort of impression of movement in the air where it had been, and then even that was gone.

I sat on the bed before my legs gave out and clasped my hands together. The light flickered, and the room was no longer silent. They weren't the sounds that had kept me up the night before: these were the same soft whispering, rustling noises the *schakalgeier* I'd encountered at my cottage had made as it brushed against the walls. The sounds I'd heard on the phone to Danie the night before – however much I'd wanted to put them down to nothing more than static on the line – had sounded very similar.

At first the noises came from the wall where I'd shone the projector, but soon they emanated from all around the room. They were in the walls, like mice: faint, but ever-present.

There was another, even more unpleasant, repetition of an experience I'd had on the night of that first encounter: a sense of pressure, as if the darkness outside had weight and substance and was pressing in on all sides. Once I was sure I heard the walls and ceiling creak.

I switched on every light in the room. That would keep them at bay, but if the power cut out – with or without the *schakalgeier's* help – I'd be defenceless. Could anything – or anyone – else help? Why hadn't Coldgrain at least tried to contact the Church? The *schakalgeier* might not be mentioned in the Bible, but if anything qualified as demonic, they did. But that wasn't much use to me tonight: I couldn't exactly order a priest from room service. And how could I convince them in time to do any good? I'd have to beg someone to come here, and what then? Anything I told them would sound insane: I'd be sectioned or locked up. And they'd turn the lights out, and what would I find standing over my bed?

No. Just get through tonight. That was all I had to do. When the sun came up, the *schakalgeier* would be gone for another day. Long enough for me to find help. Imam, priest, rabbi – even the likes of the Fraternity of Horus, if it came to it. I'd enlist anyone's help at this point.

Light was key. But I needed another line of defence, in case that failed. I remembered something, and went through Coldgrain's journal again, then rang room service to request a meal. That wasn't a bad idea anyway, as I hadn't eaten since lunch and was ravenous. But I specifically requested salt and pepper with it. The salt especially.

A small thin woman in her thirties turned up with a tray, which I gratefully took off her hands, opening the door only a crack so she wouldn't see into the room: I'd already pushed the bed as far to one side as I could and cleared a space on the floor beside it, laying out the pillows and a folded sheet. Beside that was a bottle of water, and the metal wastepaper basket in case my bladder made any demands during the night.

I ate at the writing desk in the corner of the room; then used the toilet, then went to where I'd laid the bedding out. I'd been given a plain old-fashioned salt cellar rather than a mill, thank God, and a completely full one too. Slowly, carefully, I poured what I hoped was a perfect circle around the area, then lay down in it and waited.

It wasn't long before I began to feel stupid. What would Danie make of this? What would anyone else? Imagine if the hotel staff got in here and saw what their lunatic guest was up to. Again, I saw myself being dragged away and locked up. Even after everything I'd gone through in the past weeks, even after watching the second film, it all seemed absurd. The writhing, fading shape that had pulled itself out of the wall was already becoming harder and harder to believe in. An hallucination, nothing more.

And then I was wondering if those doubts and fears were part of some kind of psychic attack by the *schakalgeier*, to make me lose faith in my own defences and make a fatal error. I'd barely been in the circle for ten minutes; it was going to be a long night. Fortunately I'd also picked up a copy of *The Radetzky March* on my travels, which would hopefully keep me occupied.

I wasn't sure if I should I try to sleep, even with the lights and the salt circle for protection. I suspected it was academic in any case, even though I was exhausted.

The *schakalgeier* rustled and whispered. The sound came first from in front, then behind, then from the left, then the right. It moved back and forth, circling.

At one point it was overhead; at another it came from the floor directly underneath me. I nearly got up and ran, but stopped myself in time.

The sound rose and fell over the next hour, until the blurred whispering gave way to a more distinct voice. It was just clear enough to recognise as one, but not enough to make out individual words. I tried to focus on the book to shut it out, but the voice droned and muttered on.

That continued for another hour, before the lights began to flicker. It was brief at first, and each incident would be separated by lengthy intervals, but as the night wore on they became more frequent, the spells of flickering would last longer, and from time to time the lights winked out completely. Only for a few seconds, but for those seconds the room would be full of darkness and the dark would begin to writhe and when that happened I shut my eyes tightly and mumbled half-remembered prayers – although more to drown out the whispering than out of any actual belief.

When the lights came back on after these episodes they blazed almost viciously bright, as if about to explode. Like the bulbs in Heggie's house had. Still, Heggie had lasted weeks. Surely tonight would be okay. But what if they were getting stronger? Heggie had cheated them, after all, but Chris hadn't. And, according to Coldgrain, they gained strength from being watched. And I'd just watched the Redbrook footage.

Another hour passed. The bathroom light went out with a loud pop. The darkness collapsed in on it as though its roof and walls had given way under a surge of debris. Whispering sounds came from the doorway. I was peripherally aware of movements in the darkness, but I didn't look; I didn't want to see.

Over the next few hours, the light over the table in the corner failed, then, in quick succession, the two bedside lamps died too. Now only the main light in the middle of the ceiling was left. It flickered but – for now – it held. Unlike the bathroom, the bedroom was still visible, but there were far more shadows now, and I avoided looking at them too. Whispers continued emanating from the blackness in the bathroom, and, less definitely, from seemingly everywhere else.

Time dragged. The light flickered. I wanted to look at my phone, but didn't dare, in case hardly any time had passed. When I did finally did, it was close to three o'clock. Four, four and a half hours till daylight. I was past the worst, I told myself.

As if in answer, the overhead light flickered again and continued to do so for several minutes. I was sure it would blow out; finally it stabilised, but was dimmer than before.

It happened again, twice, over the next hour, the bulb's strength diminishing each time. The strobe effect gave an illusion of motion to objects in the room, and made the shadowy areas twitch and expand, as if trying to reach out.

By now the sense of a felt presence had returned, along with the bitter, localised chill I knew meant a *schakalgeier* was looking directly at me. One was in the bathroom, just inside the doorway. I would easily be within its arm's reach. Only the salt circle and the failing light held it back. More shadows seemed to have accumulated in the corner near the writing desk, and they were thickening. I looked directly at them once, then refused to do so again. It wasn't so much what I saw as what I felt I was about to.

And flicker, flicker went that last light, fading and shrinking.

Somewhere between four and five a.m., the light regained its original strength, and then burned brighter still. I looked away and covered my face a second before it burst. Hot fragments speckled the backs of my hands, and the room went black.

The following hours were the longest of my life. The whisper-rustling sounds were louder than ever before, and the darkness was packed. I felt their numbers grow with every minute, closing in around their prey.

Except that I wasn't their prey, not yet. Nor was the room completely dark. The salt circle had become faintly phosphorescent, a greenish-white glow like that of an old radium watch. It illuminated the tattered lower bodies of the *schakalgeier* hovering outside it. They circled, looking for a weak point in the circle, a way in. I fumbled for the salt cellar; it was three-quarters empty, but that should be enough to close any breaches.

They couldn't get in, but continued to make noise, to the point where it should have been audible all over that floor of the hotel, although no-one came to complain or investigate. That sense of *pressure*, of the darkness squeezing tight around me like the water at the bottom of the ocean, mounted, this time applied to the insubstantial 'wall' created by the salt circle. They were trying to break through with sheer weight of numbers, and if they did it would be the end – or rather the beginning. I wished I had a knife: better Heggie's fate, or Coldgrain's, than whatever had befallen Chris. But then what about Danie? With luck she could read Coldgrain's journals, but how long would she be defenceless beforehand? If I'd only brought a pen into the circle I could at least leave a warning behind.

But I hadn't, so I just sat and stared at the floor.

My teeth were chattering; they were all staring at me. Those eyes like searchlights and a light like frost. What had Coldgrain said? *A different kind of light.* I looked up once. Shouldn't have, of course, but I'd been hoping to catch a hint of dawn through the window.

The room was packed with them. They crowded round the edges of the circle, stood or crouched on the bed. They were still, but with a kind of watchful tension, and there were so many pairs of round, pale, slowly blinking eyes.

I shut my own eyes and began again to pray as the cold intensified. Even now I don't know whether or not it gave any protection against the *schakalgeier*, but it did no harm, and helped the time pass.

It would have been easy to let sleep come, and so tempting. I was almost certain I'd still be safe inside the circle. But what if I shifted in my sleep and broke it? Even so, I might have chanced it, if the worst they could have done was kill me.

Somehow I stayed awake, and the cold begin to ease. The whispering diminished too, but I didn't open my eyes until it was almost gone. Through the open curtains I could see the grey predawn twilight outside.

Most of the *schakalgeier* had gone, conceding defeat for now, but a few still lingered in the hope of a last-minute victory. I shut my eyes and prayed, then switched to reciting poetry. Shelley, notorious atheist that he was, might not have seemed very apt, but the verse about *the obscene ravens* in *Adonais* definitely was. I was quite surprised how much of the poem I remembered.

Finally, I realised that when I closed my eyes I saw not black, but red. I risked another glance at the window, and winced. The window of my room faced east, and the rising sun shone straight through. After that long dark night, it was dazzling. But welcome.

I didn't waste time after that. I packed everything away and made for the lift, dragging the wooden chest after me. It was hard work – at one point I was sure I was about to have a cardiac, which would have been a grimly hilarious way to check out after what I'd just been through – but I didn't want to call the porter. No-one needed to see the state of my room right then. They could send me a bill for the damage later if they wanted.

The receptionist looked surprised that I wasn't staying for breakfast – I had paid for it after all – but I made an excuse about a family emergency. The only delay I allowed was her calling the porter to hump the trunk aboard the Land Rover.

I abandoned the car at the station – I'd ring the hire company as soon as I could and settle things there – and waited on the platform. I didn't trust myself to drive and from the news reports – there was a TV screen in the waiting room tuned to the twenty-four hour news – rail travel would be safer than some of the roads I'd have to take. Besides, sleep-starved as I was, I'd be a menace. Finally the train showed up and I climbed aboard.

The storm I'd encountered on my journey north had swept south-west before blowing out to sea just north of the Wash, and had wreaked worse havoc and disruption on the urban sprawls than on the isolated countryside – at least as far as public transport was concerned. The train halted about half an hour from Penrith due to flooding on the line, after which another rail replacement bus covered the rest of the journey to Sheffield by a long and winding route.

There was no wi-fi signal at any point on the journey and no phone reception either, so it was impossible to contact Danie. Later I found out that comms across the North of England had been down completely for the better part of thirty-six hours.

They were still out when I made it back to Sheffield. By the time the hackney I'd taken from the station dropped me home I was weaving and stumbling with exhaustion. Somehow I managed to drag the chest inside the house. Then I locked up, staggered to the bedroom and collapsed on the bed.

But first, I turned all the lights on, just in case I overslept. I wanted light, bright and clear and plenty of it, scouring every corner of the cottage. I suppose I should have drawn a salt circle around the bed too, but I hadn't the energy.

———

Switching on the lights, as it turned out, had been a good idea, because it was getting dark when I finally woke. A hot shower helped, followed by a stir-fry slung together from whatever I could find in cans, followed by a mug of strong, sweet tea.

While the kettle boiled, I switched on the television and booted up the laptop. There was extensive flood and storm damage across the country, together with a red tide staining almost the entire English Channel and causing dead fish to wash up bloated rotten and stinking on beaches from Coverack to Hastings and the Scillies to St Helier. Fresh rioting had broken out in Hull and Dover; in Birmingham, racists had set several streets populated by ethnic minorities and migrants ablaze. Shootings in Belfast; the army on the streets in Newcastle again.

London was the usual freakshow and carnival of stabbings, shootings, gangs of one political, religious or just plain hooliganistic stripe or another roaming the streets. Nothing about Islington that I could see, although it might easily be lost in the chaos. I wondered how many *schakalgeier* might hover, unseen, above the dying and the dead tonight.

I googled *Islington, incident, woman* and finally just entered Danie's name, but found nothing. Hopefully no news was good news.

That was when my phone started buzzing. Mostly email alerts and texts, and most of them from Danie. I grabbed my laptop and fired it up, entering my email on it while opening the texts on the phone.

You okay? Not heard from you. Any luck in the Lakes? Ash? You okay?

ASH! EARTH CALLING! WHAT THE FUCK'S GOING ON UP THERE?

Shit. Just seen the 'net's down oop North. That's what happens when you leave civilisation I guess lol jk. FFS call me when you see this.

Okay, got something. Might be a lead. Sending you a scan of it in a sec.

I consulted the emails. She'd sent three, all with attachments. I opened up the earliest one.

Hi hun, (it began)

So my police contact came through for me again. Remember how they ID'd Coldgrain through stuff he had on him? Turns out that included things like his passport and driver's licence, but he had some letters too. All his ID was in a sealed waterproof wallet, so it was all in perfect condition. Got them scanned and sent over.

Anyway, remember the Institute for Psychic, Theosophical and Metaphysical Enquiry? The last group to own Redbrook House? Turns out they did reply to Coldgrain after all. Last letter turns up just before he did a flit from his lab. Some useful info there.

I hope you're okay, mate. Worried. Not heard from you. Mail me back ASAP. Or ring me. Text. Something. Okay?

The D. x

It was nice to be needed, even if only out of desperation. I opened up the scans Danie had attached and tried to ring her, but her phone went straight to her answering service. I told it that I was alive and well and had got her emails, and I'd speak to her soon. Maybe she'd passed a night like mine and was still asleep. I hoped so.

I told myself I was worrying unnecessarily and began to study the scans. The first was from a Mrs Theresa Prisk, the General Secretary of the Coleflax Parapsychological Society – apparently a successor organisation to the IPTME. It was short and terse and didn't provide anything of much interest. Mrs Prisk informed Coldgrain that while she herself had no information about events at Redbrook House, as the relevant files had been among a number of the Institute's records destroyed in the Blitz, she had forwarded his letter on to her mother, Mrs Lucinda Coleflax, who had been the Secretary at the time that Redbrook had belonged to the Institute.

The second letter offered a bit more substance, although the tone was guarded:

———

1st May, 1959

Dear Mr Coldgrain,

Thank your for your letter of the 10th December, 1958, the substance of which my daughter Mrs Prisk has relayed to me. Please accept my apologies for failing to reply sooner: I live abroad these days and lead a somewhat peripatetic existence, so I am hard to reach.

Regarding your query: the Institute's ownership of Redbrook House was comparatively brief. Our intention was to substantiate reports of psychic phenomena in that location and, if possible, to dispel or lay them to rest. In this, we were not successful.

That, of course, is no more than the baldest possible summation of what transpired. However, for various reasons, it is an episode that I am reluctant to discuss in greater detail without good cause.

I would appreciate it, therefore, if you could enlighten me as to the nature of your interest in the Redbrook House, and as to your intentions with regard to any further details of the business that I might impart.

You may write to me directly at the attached correspondence address. I telephone them regularly, and they will relay the contents of your missive to me when I do. It will be substantially quicker than attempting to contact me via Mrs Prisk. I mention this in case your need for information regarding Redbrook is of a particularly urgent nature.

Yours,

Lucinda Coleflax (Mrs)

The last paragraph of the letter might have been a hint of some kind: if so, Coldgrain definitely responded to it. There's no copy of the letter he wrote, but it looks as though he replied almost by return of post, and told Mrs Coleflax all. Her second letter was much longer than the first.

17th May 1959

Dear Mr Coldgrain,

Thank you for your letter of the 8th. I'm truly sorry to hear of your troubles, and only wish I'd had your letter sooner; I might have been able to spare you some distress.

I wish that I could reply to you with more hopeful news, but as you will know yourself by now, any attempt to beard the schakalgeier in their den can only worsen an already bleak situation. The unpalatable truth of the matter is that, having attached themselves to a living subject, the schakalgeier are impossible to dislodge and will continue to plague the unlucky sufferer. It is, if you like, a chronic affliction, and the only remedies are palliative in nature. Of the IPTME members involved in the Redbrook investigation, only I remain. The others are dead – the fortunate ones are, at least. Your surmises regarding the schakalgeier's intentions are, I'm afraid, all too accurate.

Nonetheless, I have remained on this side both of the grave and of whatever plane the schakalgeier – I do like that word and have fallen oddly in love with it, as you can tell; I'm rather envious of you for having coined the term! – inhabit, so, given that I'm still here thirty years after my encounter with them, those remedies can be highly efficacious.

You're already aware of two effective means of defence, which are the salt circle and God's good light. It says a great deal for your determination and strength of character that you have held out against them for as long as you have armed with these weapons alone, but as you'll already have discovered, their assaults on you will now redouble following your intrusion at Redbrook.

Fortunately, other weapons may be added to your arsenal. There are a number of talismans and materials that for whatever reason can also repel the schakalgeier, and you'll find these appended to the substance of this letter.

However, the most effective deterrent against them is also one of the simplest, and one you have yet to avail yourself of.

I liken the schakalgeier, in some respects, to bloodhounds: that is, having got your 'scent', they will pursue you quite relentlessly, to the end of your days. I've found no way to permanently shake them off, and if there is a point at which they lose interest and abandon the chase, they're yet to reach it with me even after thirty years. However, if you're always in the same place, it won't take long for the bloodhounds to come to you.

We are told that 'fight or flight' is the instinctive reaction to a threat: you've explored the possibilities of one, but not the other. I believed I mentioned in my previous letter that I lead a somewhat peripatetic existence. Although I will admit that I have enjoyed seeing the world, this has not been a matter of choice on my part. Simply put, since 1937 I have not remained in one fixed location for any period in excess of a fortnight.

You have remained based in the same location for some considerable time, Mr Coldgrain with the result that the schakalgeier who have attached themselves to you can home readily in on your scent. If you take stock of your own experiences I think you'll realise you've been less troubled by them when you have been away from your home, particularly when you've visited a hitherto unfamiliar location.

As I say, you'll never rid yourself of them entirely: that is important to realise, and to accept. But by regularly relocating yourself, you will keep them at bay. Through trial and error I have determined that two weeks is the maximum safe period I can remain in one spot. (Even within this period, it is advisable to make use of the other defences you have: once or twice they have caught up with me earlier than that and forced me to relocate before I had intended.)

I'm painfully aware that one's ability to remain in constant flight is to some extent constrained by age, health and financial situation. I can offer no assistance there, as both my finances and my general vitality are limited. Neither are exhausted yet, but it's fair to say that they almost certainly will be well within the next decade. When that point is reached, the possibilities of both fight and flight will have been exhausted, and there will be only option remaining. At any cost, we _must_ avoid being taken alive by the schakalgeier.

I hope this is some help to you; I appreciate, too, that what I prescribe can offer little more than bare survival. It will be, of necessity, a somewhat lonely existence, but if one does not mind solitude, that need not be intolerable. In the words of the late Mr Buchan, it's a great life if you don't weaken. Or at least a good one.

That, anyway, is my recipe for survival. Only you can decide if it's worth the cost, and how long for. You're more than welcome to write again, whatever that may be worth. It is always pleasant to communicate with another who shares one's own predicament.

I wish you the best possible fortune.
With all good wishes,
Lucinda Coleflax (Mrs)

The appendix to the letter contained a number of symbols that could be chalked on walls and floors, together with a list of other materials that could form a protective barrier – copper or iron wire, certain kinds of herbs. Mrs Coleflax recommended Coldgrain keep a supply of these with him at all times, so that he'd always be able to set up a rudimentary defence if caught out at night away from 'home'.

It was a pretty gruelling and radical lifestyle change, and as she said, it was a moot point how much you'd actually have left to live for. Coldgrain obviously hadn't thought it worth his while to continue for long, if at all. He could have died within weeks or even days of that last letter, or eked out some kind of nomadic existence for a year or two, but either way, he'd soon decided that it wasn't worthwhile.

I wondered if I'd be able to take it – if Danie would. Or, perhaps, the two of us together.

That prompted me to call her again, but again the phone went to the answering service, so I started scrolling through the storm of text messages she'd sent me instead.

You okay? Jesus, Ash, you'd better be. FFS CALL ME WHEN YOU GET THIS.

Ash, things have been starting to get weird around here. I don't know what's happened, but it's as if they're stepping things up.

Did you know Coldgrain came up with a name for them? Called them schakalgeier. Suits the fucking horrible things.

Do you want to know what I'm doing right now? No, not that, get your mind out of the bloody gutter you dirty sod.

I'm sitting on my living room floor in the middle of a SALT CIRCLE. I saw there was something about that in the letter from Mrs Coleflax. Had a look for some of the herbs she was talking about but I don't have anything like that in the spice rack. She mentions garlic, though. I've got some garlic granules so I've sprinkled some of those around. Just hope nobody calls round. Never live it down.

Yeah, I know, that's daft isn't it? Got a lot more to worry about than that.

I've got every light in the house on, but I think they're starting to go. I've heard a few pings, like bulbs blowing out. This is what happened to Heggie, isn't it?

Oh fuck. What time is it? How long before it's light?

Shit. I'm sorry about this. Your inbox is gonna look insane tomorrow. Filled up with this shit. I'll be embarrassed. Look do me a favour and delete all these okay? I'm just doing them right now because I'm going mad in here.

I mean, here I am, sitting in the middle of all this black magic or occult or whatever it is crap trying to keep safe from those bloody THINGS out there AND I'M LIVETEXTING YOU ALL ABOUT IT. That's a perfect symbol of something or other isn't it?

SHIT

Kitchen light just went.

Hall light's gone out too.

Bulb overhead's starting to flicker.

Shit shit shit.

I can hear them. Whispering and rustling. In the dark. I can see the dark moving. The light in here's still on but I don't know how long fuck

Light's gone out.

Ash, I'm bloody scared. Wish you were here. Nothing you can do I know. Nothing anyone can. Just might help somehow. But maybe you're going through this as well. Can you imagine? The two of us talking each other through this.

The salt circle's glowing. I'm serious. I wish it wasn't. I mean, it means I've got a bit of light in here but I can see them and they're fucking horrible.

i'm so scared. i'm so scared

I just want to get through tonight. Just let me get through tonight and then we'll see. I've got a bag packed, you know. Right next to me. Just in case. I should have legged it. Gone somewhere. I've been stuck here and you've been on the move. That's probably helped you a bit.

How long till daylight now?

That was the last text, but it wasn't the last message. At that point, a notification came through on my phone – an answerphone message, from Danie.

It had been sent in the early hours of the morning, just after the final text.

"Ash? Ash? You there? Fuck sake pick up if you are. Jesus. Can you hear them?"

I could. Those whispers. I sometimes think a good sound engineer might be able to filter them out from the message, clean up and amplify them, tell me what they were saying. But would I really want that? If everything that had happened so far was any clue, that would only make things worse.

"Not sure what time it is right now," she said. "Hang on." She breathed out. "About three a.m. Not too long till dawn. If I can just last it out I'll be okay."

Indistinct background sounds and an indrawn breath from Danie that was close to a scream.

"Oh fuck oh fuck oh fuck they're right up against the circle like they're trying to push through. It'll hold won't it? It'll hold, it'll hold. Just a bit longer. Bit longer. Few more hours."

She was breathing fast, nearly hyperventilating. She sounded close to tears. So alone and so afraid: I gripped the phone so hard I heard the casing creak.

"Fucking phone's nearly out of juice. Only charged it up this morning. Just let me get through this. Just let me get through it. FUCK. There's so many of the bastard things."

The whispering and the rustling was very loud now, and there was static and interference on the line.

"I'm sorry, Ash. I'm so fucking sorry. I lo—"

And that was where it ended.

I tried ringing her back, but I didn't expect her to answer.

And she didn't.

Later that night, in response to my telephone call, two police officers went to the house on Barrowford Row.

The front door was open. In the living room, a circle had been drawn on the floor in ordinary table salt, and odd symbols had been chalked on the walls. A mobile phone, later identified as Danie's, lay inside the circle. The screen was cracked, and the electronics had burned out.

The house, otherwise was empty.

Every lightbulb in the building had exploded.

———

I sold the cottage, and I've kept on the move ever since. The advantage of my profession, after all, is that wherever I lay my laptop is home, so in some ways becoming a nomad is less of a disruption than it might have been to Victor Coldgrain. I had some savings, following the payment from Chris. One good thing to come out of the mess.

It's a very different world to the one that either Lucinda Coleflax or Victor Coldgrain knew, but Mrs Coleflax managed to keep one step ahead of the *schakalgeier* throughout the full term of the Second World War, so I'm not too discouraged. Her advice to Coldgrain to always have the basics of protection on him has saved me more than once: there was the time the riots in Guildford trapped me on a train carriage overnight. I got some strange looks, sprinkling salt around myself like that, but I can live with it. I tend not to use public transport any more, especially since I started spending more time abroad; I overcame my aversion to driving long distances, bought a good, sturdy 4X4 and keep a tent in the back. So far it's served me well. Storms, floods, and near outright civil war: none of them has caught me unprepared so far.

I wouldn't be here if they had. The *schakalgeier* are as patient as they are relentless. And as watchful for any mistake.

I've had time to do a little more research, to try and tie up a few loose ends. One small piece of local news – meaningless out of context – mentioned the unexplained disappearance of Father Roger Berrison, a Catholic priest, in 1961. There had been screams and sounds of a struggle reported from his church on the night in question, and the police were anxious to trace a man in his sixties who'd been seen in Berrison's company that night. I realised I had no idea what Victor Coldgrain had looked like, but Paddy sent me a photograph of a thin-faced, balding man whose remaining hair was iron-grey. It matched the police description.

Further checking revealed that no trace of Father Berrison, alive or dead, had been found in the sixty years since. I haven't entirely ruled out seeking religious aid, but it doesn't seem to have done Coldgrain any good. Maybe, like him, I'll consider it as a last roll of the dice, when all other options are exhausted. Or maybe I shouldn't consider it at all. Limit the damage, not drag anyone else down with me.

Despite my desire never to see him again, I did have cause to contact Mr Lloyd once more. In response to my enquiry, he told me that yes, he did still have the Harrach glass jug, and named his price for it. I paid it, and he sent it to me.

The Harrach jug is currently in a secure storage space, along with any other effects I couldn't take with me, sell or bear to give up. I still haven't opened the cardboard box he sent it in, so there it lies, sealed amidst the packing chips. Given the kind of stuff Mr Lloyd liked to trade in, it's entirely possible there might be an unexpected and unwanted free gift attached to it, but I don't think so. That's not why I haven't opened it, anyway. It's because, quite simply, it isn't for me.

Danielle Starmer is still listed as missing. I often think about what she'd been about to say before she was cut off. I know what I want it to have been. What I hope it was. But then, I was always a romantic, and she wasn't. Besides, I think she'd only have made a confession like that if she knew there was no hope, if she'd seen them breaking through.

And I know, more than likely, that's what happened. I know it is. But I keep hoping that maybe she got away. Her door was open, after all. And they never found the bag she said she'd packed.

I still send the occasional forlorn message to her email address or through this or that social media app, usually in the maudlin early hours of some drunken sleepless morning. And sometimes I search for her online, looking for anything, any clue that might tell me she's still in this world, if not where.

She may still be out there, somewhere. I tell myself she may have reasons for avoiding contact with me – fear, perhaps, that it would bring the *schakalgeier's* attentions down on us both. Or perhaps she's just concerned with her own preservation; as I said, she always had a ruthlessness I lacked. I'd rather believe that, even if I never see her again.

The alternative: yes, I know the alternative. I know where she most probably is now. What purpose she's serving, I have no idea. Food, entertainment, a means of propagating their kind. Or – given the *schakalgeier's* fundamentally unknowable nature – she might even be one of them now. They might be our afterlife – unless of course she's been robbed even of that by being snatched into their domain alive.

Round and round they go, possibilities and speculations, and they give me no peace.

And so I carry on. I move whenever there are whispers and rustles in the dark, or when the darkness seems to move with a little more purpose than usual, or whenever I glimpse things in it like pale, blinking eyes. It can be tiring; sometimes the desire to just… *stop*… and let things take their course is alluring beyond description. Sometimes – when I'm certain that they have her and are tormenting her endlessly – I'm actually tempted to switch off the lights and brush away the salt circle, toss away the herbs, unravel my barriers of wire and wipe the chalk symbols from the walls. Where there's life, there's hope, after all. Even in whatever place the *schakalgeier* – and Danie too, perhaps – live. The hope of companionship, for example, with a fellow captive. Or – nothing is impossible – even of escape.

But, for now, I hold; I wait, and I listen to the dark. And I watch the shadows.

Acknowledgements

As ever, thanks are due first and foremost to my beloved Cate Gardner for listening to the first draft of *A Different Kind of Light*, (thankfully no dogs, fictional or otherwise, were harmed this time around,) and for putting up with me and my nonsense generally. You make my life so much better, love.

Major thanks and gratitude are also due to Danie Ware for letting me steal her first name for a character in this. No resemblance to that awesome person and writer is intended or should be inferred.

I'm also very grateful to Sarah Lotz for her amazing cover blurb, and for some hilarious email exchanges.

Thanks as well to my brother from another mother Gary McMahon for reading the second draft of this and for providing another excellent quote.

The authors of *The World's Worst Disasters of the Twentieth Century*, where I first read about the Le Mans Disaster and started this ball rolling, way back around the beginning of the 21st century.

The huge number of bloggers and review sites who've helped spread the word about my work. It is hugely appreciated. These include (but are not limited to): This Is Horror, Ginger Nuts of Horror, Kendall Reviews, Runalong The Shelves, The Future Fire, Sci-Fi and Scary, Hellnotes, Rachel Verkade, Ross Warren, Marc Francis, Daisy Lyle and countless others. I hugely appreciate your kindness and support.

Thank you as well to Priya Sharma and Mark Greenwood, Hannah Dennerly, Lynda E. Rucker, Gemma Files, Roberta Lannes-Sealey and countless other friends, on social media and otherwise, who've given me encouragement and support when times were tough and spirits low. Again, I appreciate every one of you.

I'm also enormously grateful, once again, to Steve Shaw of Black Shuck Books, of course, for bringing this twisted child of mine into the world.

Finally, my thanks to all the readers who've supported my work over the years.

Once again, I can't shake the feeling that I've forgotten to thank someone important. If so, I apologise: hopefully I'll remember you next time...

Simon Bestwick was born in Wolverhampton, bred in Manchester, and now lives on the Wirral while pining for Wales. He is the author of six novels, four full-length short story collections and has been four times shortlisted for the British Fantasy Award. He is married to long-suffering fellow author Cate Gardner, and still hasn't kicked his addictions to Pepsi Max or semicolons. His latest books are the collection *And Cannot Come Again*, from Horrific Tales Publishing, and his novella *Roth-Steyr*, also published by Black Shuck Books. He posts new fiction every month at patreon.com/SimonBestwick

THE THREE BOOKS

by

Paul StJohn Mackintosh

"I've been told that this is the most elegant thing I've ever written. I can't think how such a dark brew of motifs came together to create that effect. But there's unassuaged longing and nostalgia in here, interwoven with the horror, as well as an unflagging drive towards the final consummation. I still feel more for the story's characters, whether love or loathing, than for any others I've created to date. Tragedy, urban legend, Gothic romance, warped fairy tale of New York: it's all there. And of course, most important of all is the seductive allure of writing and of books – and what that can lead some people to do.

You may not like my answer to the mystery of the third book. But I hope you stay to find out."

Paul StJohn Mackintosh

———•———

"Paul StJohn Mackintosh is one of those writers who just seems to quietly get on with the business of producing great fiction... it's an excellent showcase for his obvious talents. His writing, his imagination, his ability to lay out a well-paced and intricate story in only 100 pages is a great testament to his skills."

—This is Horror

BLACK STAR, BLACK SUN

by

Rich Hawkins

"Black Star, Black Sun *is my tribute to Lovecraft, Ramsey Campbell, and the haunted fields of Somerset, where I seemed to spend much of my childhood. It's a story about going home and finding horror there when something beyond human understanding begins to invade our reality. It encompasses broken dreams, old memories, lost loved ones and a fundamentally hostile universe. It's the last song of a dying world before it falls to the Black Star."*

Rich Hawkins

"Black Star, Black Sun *possesses a horror energy of sufficient intensity to make readers sit up straight. A descriptive force that shifts from the raw to the nuanced. A ferocious work of macabre imagination and one for readers of Conrad Williams and Gary McMahon."*
—Adam Nevill, author of *The Ritual*

"Reading Hawkins' novella is like sitting in front of a guttering open fire. Its glimmerings captivate, hissing with irrepressible life, and then, just when you're most seduced by its warmth, it spits stinging embers your way. This is incendiary fiction. Read at arms' length."
—Gary Fry, author of *Conjure House*

blackshuckbooks.co.uk/signature

DEAD LEAVES

by

Andrew David Barker

"*This book is my love letter to the horror genre. It is about what it means to be a horror fan; about how the genre can nurture an adolescent mind; how it can be a positive force in life.*

This book is set during a time when horror films were vilified in the press and in parliament like never before. It is about how being a fan of so-called 'video nasties' made you, in the eyes of the nation, a freak, a weirdo, or worse, someone who could actually be a danger to society.

This book is partly autobiographical, set in a time when Britain seemed to be a war with itself. It is a working class story about hope. All writers, filmmakers, musicians, painters – artists of any kind –were first inspired to create their own work by the guiding light of another's. The first spark that sets them on their way.

This book is about that spark."

Andrew David Barker

"*Whilst Thatcher colluded with the tabloids to distract the public... an urban quest for the ultimate video nasty was unfolding, before the forces of media madness and power drunk politicians destroyed the Holy Grail of gore!*"

—Graham Humphreys, painter of *The Evil Dead* poster

blackshuckbooks.co.uk/signature

Also from BLACK SHUCK *Signature*

THE FINITE
by
Kit Power

"The Finite *started as a dream; an image, really, on the edge of waking. My daughter and I, joining a stream of people walking past our house. We were marching together, and I saw that many of those behind us were sick, and struggling, and then I looked to the horizon and saw the mushroom cloud. I remember a wave of perfect horror and despair washing over me; the sure and certain knowledge that our march was doomed, as were we.*

The image didn't make it into the story, but the feeling did. King instructs us to write about what scares us. In The Finite, *I wrote about the worst thing I can imagine; my own childhood nightmare, resurrected and visited on my kid.*"

Kit Power

"The Finite *is* Where the Wind Blows *or* Threads *for the 21st century, played out on a tight scale by a father and his young daughter, which only serves to make it all the more heartbreaking.*"

—Priya Sharma, author of *Ormeshadow*

blackshuckbooks.co.uk/signature

RICOCHET

by

Tim Dry

"With Ricochet *I wanted to break away from the traditional linear form of storytelling in a novella and instead create a series of seemingly unrelated vignettes. Like the inconsistent chaos of vivid dreams I chose to create stand-alone episodes that vary from being fearful to blackly humorous to the downright bizarre. It's a book that you can dip into at any point but there is an underlying cadence that will carry you along, albeit in a strangely seductive new way.*

Prepare to encounter a diverse collection of characters. Amongst them are gangsters, dead rock stars, psychics, comic strip heroes and villains, asylum inmates, UFOs, occult nazis, parisian ghosts, decaying and depraved royalty and topping the bill a special guest appearance by the Devil himself."

Tim Dry

Reads like the exquisite lovechild of William Burroughs and Philip K. Dick's fiction, with some Ballard thrown in for good measure. Wonderfully imaginative, darkly satirical - this is a must read!

—Paul Kane, author of *Sleeper(s)* and *Ghosts*

ROTH-STEYR

by

Simon Bestwick

"*You never know which ideas will stick in your mind, let alone where they'll go. Roth-Steyr began with an interest in the odd designs and names of early automatic pistols, and the decision to use one of them as a story title. What started out as an oddball short piece became a much longer and darker tale about how easily a familiar world can fall apart, how old convictions vanish or change, and why no one should want to live forever.*

It's also about my obsession with history, in particular the chaotic upheavals that plagued the first half of the twentieth century and that are waking up again. Another 'long dark night of the European soul' feels very close today.

So here's the story of Valerie Varden. And her Roth-Steyr."

Simon Bestwick

———•———

"*A slice of pitch-black cosmic pulp, elegant and inventive in all the most emotionally engaging ways.*"

—Gemma Files, author of *In That Endlessness, Our End*

blackshuckbooks.co.uk/signature